Sister, Daughter, Mother, Wife

Lilian Kendrick

ACKNOWLEDGMENTS

Thank you to all the friends and family who have encouraged me throughout the process of writing this book.

Special thanks are due to those 'strong women' – you know who you are – who have been my inspiration for many years.

DEDICATION

To Gillian McKinley (RIP)
A dear friend, sadly missed.

COVER DESIGN

The cover was designed and photographed by my niece
Veronica Deery – Autumn 2008

Chapter One

When did it happen? What did I miss?
When did this routine replace wedded bliss?
When did your heart leave? And where did it go?
I guess there are answers that I'll never know.

(from Josie's Journal-"Cards for all Occasions")

Josie ran through the rain shivering. She could hear the phone ringing and cursed as she dropped her keys in a puddle. Inside, the ringing stopped as her hand touched the receiver. She checked 1471 and an automated voice informed her that the last person who called withheld their number.

"Damn!" she moaned, pushing her wet hair away from her face and rubbing her tired eyes, aware that she really needed to get a good night's sleep. It had been a long time, too long, since she had been able to relax.

She made some strong coffee to revive herself for now, and hoped she would be lucky enough to get an early night if Rick was in a good mood, and Susie was in independent mode; two situations which rarely coincided.

Glancing at the clock, she realised that her afternoon off had dwindled away. It was already three-thirty. Susie would be home from college in half an hour and Rick would be back from the office at six. Perhaps she had time to take a quick bath.

The sound of the phone interrupted her thoughts, and with a sigh Josie picked up the receiver, somehow knowing that any hope of a restful half-hour had now flown away.

"Is that Mrs. Anson? Mrs Josie Anson?"

"Yes"

"I'm calling from Firton Police Station. Can you confirm that you are acquainted with a Mr. Lee Andrews?"

Josie took a deep breath before replying.

"Yes, he's my brother. Has something happened to him? Is he OK?"

"He's asleep in one of our holding cells, madam. He was picked up by one of our beat officers earlier this afternoon, drunk and confused on the High Street."

"Can I come and see him?"

"I'd be glad if you would. If you come and collect him it would save a great deal of time and resources. On this occasion we won't be pressing charges, but we do have to ensure that he is returned to a place of safety when he leaves our custody."

"I'll be there in fifteen minutes. Thank you, officer."

Leaving a scribbled note for Susie, Josie grabbed her keys and handbag and rushed out. It was still raining heavily and she hadn't brought her coat, so she was wet through by the time she reached the car, parked on the road, leaving the driveway clear for Rick.

By the time she reached the police station, and dashed from the car park to the reception, she was conscious that her white sweater had become almost transparent and was clinging to her body like a second skin. Making her way to the desk, she felt embarrassed and self-conscious. Perhaps she should have taken the time to tidy herself up a bit. What were they going to think of her – the bedraggled sister of the drunk? Oh well, it was too late to worry about it now, and anyway, what did it matter as long as they let her take Lee away from here?

In the small room that they called a holding cell, Lee lay curled up on a sort of camp bed. He seemed to be sleeping soundly and for a moment as she looked down at him, she wondered how it had come to this. What had turned her brilliant, beautiful, witty little brother into this sad dysfunctional man? Why was it that the once most popular kid in town was now so alone that the only number on his SIM card was hers?

He looked dishevelled, but clean, so she guessed this drinking session hadn't gone on for too long. Sometimes they lasted days, but he'd always avoided getting involved with the police before, because he usually managed to make his own way home. He looked childlike sleeping there. His once full and rounded face showed signs of the alcoholism that had enslaved him for the last few years. His cheeks were marked with a network of broken veins producing an unnatural redness against the weary pallor of the rest of his face.

Josie sighed, remembering how handsome he used to be. She reached out and touched his hair. That at least had not changed too much. He still wore it quite long, curling around his collar. A few strands of grey were starting to appear, but mostly it was the same jet black that it had always been.

Lee stirred and opened his eyes. A broad grin spread across his face when he saw Josie. He tried to sit up, but couldn't quite make it.

"Sis," he said, his speech only slightly slurred. "How did you find me? Even I don't know where I am."

"Sibling radar." She replied, handing him his mobile phone. "I'm still the only number in your phone book so they took a chance that I knew you. The desk sergeant gave me your stuff." She had his keys and wallet in her hand.

"Who did? Oh yeah, I remember - the police. They rescued me from something or other. My head hurts. Did someone hit me?"

"Mr. Smirnoff, I'm guessing. Come on; let's get you out of here." She helped him to sit up and put on his trainers and duffle coat. Walking out, with Lee leaning on her shoulder for support she thanked the officer on duty for his kindness.

The rain seemed to bring Lee to his senses and he seemed to relish its refreshing coldness.

"I guess I screwed up again, didn't I?" he asked.

Josie didn't reply, she just unlocked the passenger door of the car, helped him in and made sure his seat belt was fastened, before walking round to get in the other side. Lee seemed dismayed by her lack of response and he put his hand on hers as she put the key in the ignition.

"I love you, Sis." he said. "You know that don't you?"

"Yes, and I love you too, but God alone knows why!" At this, Lee laughed heartily and it wasn't long before she was laughing too as she drove him home and dropped him off at his flat.

It was five-fifteen when Josie let herself into the house at last. Rock music was blasting from a music channel on the TV, and Susie lay sprawled across an armchair. Her bag was dumped in the middle of the floor and her coat had been deposited in a heap on the sofa. She looked up when her mother came in, and reading the signs, picked up the remote and lowered the volume.

"Coffee?" she asked, getting up and heading for the kitchen.

"Cheers, love." Josie busied herself with picking up her daughter's scattered belongings and restoring order to the room. Then, joining Susie in the kitchen, she searched the freezer for something she could produce for dinner in half an hour.

"How was Uncle Lee?" Susie asked as she placed the coffee on the table.

"It's a long story." Josie replied. "He's OK now though, I think." There was a tremor in her voice that Susie couldn't fail to notice. She hugged her mother.

"I don't know how you do it, Mum. More to the point, I don't know why you do it. You're always running around looking after someone." Josie returned the hug.

"You'll understand one day. Now can you put some pasta on while I sling a Bolognese together? Your dad's another one that needs looking after."

*

At nine o'clock Josie tried calling Rick's mobile for the third time. It was still switched off. He hadn't come home for dinner, and he hadn't called. Not that this was the first time, but it was a long time since he'd done anything like this. Josie poured herself a large vodka and drank it neat. She could hear the sound of Susie's CD player from upstairs.

Her thoughts returned to Rick. She wasn't worried in the usual sense. She didn't think she should be calling the hospitals or anything like that. He wouldn't have been involved in an accident. More likely an "urgent" meeting had been called with some client or other. At least that would be the story he told, if he even bothered to explain himself. Would this client be young and blonde like the last one? Josie could almost taste the bitterness of the memory.

Susie was just six months old when Josie found out about Rick's first affair. He had been working late every evening for weeks and disappearing for hours at weekends. Then the letter had arrived.

"Who is she, Rick? Is this what you mean by 'working late'?" She threw the letter onto the table as Rick sat down for dinner. She'd meant to wait until later, but it had been eating away at her all afternoon. Rick read in silence and then crumpled the letter and threw it across the kitchen.

"Rubbish!" he announced. "You can't tell me you believe this crap. It's just someone trying to cause trouble."

"I want to believe you, but she knows so much detail. How does she know so much?" Josie was sobbing now as she thought about the revelations the letter contained. The writer had spared no details of her alleged assignations with Rick. The dates, the times...they all fitted in with times when Rick had not been at home. Rick rose from to his feet and took Josie by the shoulders.

"If I tell you it's not true, then it's not true and that's all there is to it, understand? I'm your husband, the father of

your child, and you'd rather believe some poisonous piece of filth! How dare you accuse me of this?" He shook her back and forth, as he spoke. "Now, put all this nonsense out of your head and we won't talk about it again." He let go of her shoulders as he calmed down. Josie looked at her husband, the father of her child, and decided to believe him. It would be easier that way.

Much later, Josie awoke to the sound of the front door closing, followed by Rick's footsteps as he came upstairs. She waited and listened as he walked past the slightly open door of their bedroom and went into the spare room. Hearing the door close, Josie felt her heart sink. She knew it was happening again and she sobbed silently into her pillow until she drifted back to sleep.

When the alarm clock sounded at half-past six, Josie was momentarily disorientated. Her sleep had hardly been restful and she lay for a few minutes trying to remember what day it was. She could hear the shower running and realised that she had to get up quickly if she were to see Rick before he left the house. At times like these he would try to avoid her for as long as possible. It was the closest he ever came to showing any feelings of guilt. She threw on her dressing gown and went down to the kitchen to make coffee and wait for him to put in an appearance. When he came down, five minutes later, he was taken aback to see her sitting at the table.

"Good morning love." She tried to sound unperturbed "I missed you last night."

Rick concentrated on pouring himself a cup of coffee to avoid eye contact. "It was a very late meeting; I didn't want to disturb you."

"Will you be home for dinner tonight?" She was determined not to make this too easy for him. "I thought I might do a roast."

Rick didn't reply. He drank his coffee and stared out of the window. Josie watched him, willing him to turn around, but knowing he would not. She waited and then rising from the table, she took her coffee through to the living-room and switched on the TV to catch the early morning news. As Rick opened the front door a few moments later, she called after him.

"Could you at least call me to let me know if you'll want dinner?"

The door closed firmly as Rick left without replying. Josie bit her lip and wondered why this kept happening. Yes, Rick was moody, but he was always moody. He was naturally selfish and spoiled. His mother had seen to that; but to be fair, Josie knew that throughout the twenty years of their marriage she had done little to change him. She had found out in the early years that it was far easier to give in to him than to suffer the misery of disagreeing with him over small things.

Once Susie was born, Rick had cast her in the role of housewife and mother with no opinions other than domestic ones. He stopped conversing with her on any subject outside of home and family, and her attempts at expressing her views were silenced by his cold response. He adored his beautiful baby, but his wife was there to cook his meals, wash his clothes, look after his child and be sexually compliant.

Even in their most intimate moments, Josie was not allowed to express her needs or desires. Any sign of her taking the initiative would lead eventually to a tirade of accusations and verbal abuse; but only after he had taken his satisfaction and left her feeling cheap and emotionally bruised. Sometimes the bruising had been more tangible, but never where it could be seen. On such occasions Rick would be semi-apologetic to begin with and then move on to explain gently that if she hadn't struggled, or complained or said this or that, then she wouldn't have been hurt. So it had

11

been an accident, but one for which she must take responsibility, and of course, it would never happen again. Not until the next time.

The news gave way to the weather forecast and hearing that snow was expected within the hour, Josie roused herself to get ready for work. She called Susie and told her to keep the radio tuned to the local station in case the college declared a "snow day". In these enlightened and high-tech times, it only took a couple of inches of the white stuff to throw the city into complete chaos. Josie however had no desire to stay at home today, so she left the house half an hour earlier than usual to make the ten minute drive to the office.

Chapter Two

Josie was reasonably cheerful as she arrived at work. She loved her job as a verse-writer for a small firm of printers. It gave her a chance to be creative and witty. Two attributes which were not encouraged at home. She and Pam had been hired by *"Jasuprint"* six months ago as a sort of experiment. The firm used to design and print invitations, flyers and advertising literature for local businesses and individuals, but they had decided to branch out into the field of greetings cards produced under their own label. Pam was a skilled cartoonist and Josie had a proven flair for verse and both were returning to the employment market after a long time. They worked well together and enjoyed each other's company, sharing a sense of humour and a need to be out of the house. The cards were proving to be quite popular locally, and the two women had recently been asked to sign permanent contracts; a situation which had pleased them both immensely.

As the first to arrive, Josie unlocked the office she shared with Pam. She glanced across the hallway and saw that Jas hadn't arrived yet. His door was closed and there was no light showing through the frosted glass panel above it. She guessed he must be caught in traffic as the snow was now falling quite heavily. She hung her coat on the stand behind the door and switched on the computers on her desk and Pam's.

Josie set the coffee-maker in motion, and sat down at the computer to start work. Opening her email she found the usual collection of SPAM and only one real message. It was from Jas.

Hi Jo,
Guessing you'll be there before Pam. Exciting news may follow – will be out of the office all morning at a meeting. We'll all need a working lunch when I get back. Order pizza for 1pm. (Remember mine's veggie.) Put it on the account. – No slacking!
LOL
Jas.

Josie wondered what the exciting news might be. She liked Jas; he was a considerate boss with a good sense of humour. He was so enthusiastic that people working with him couldn't fail to respond. Pam often said that he ran the business for fun, as it was hardly a great profit-maker, although the company managed to keep its head above water. His middle-class English education, combined with his Indian background and culture made him an extremely good negotiator in terms of securing contracts amongst the small multicultural businesses in Birmingham.

The door burst open and Pam stormed in, pulling off her coat and throwing it over the back of her chair.

"That selfish bastard," she always referred to her ex-husband that way, "rang me just as I was leaving the house. He's getting married again. I can't imagine why he thought I needed to know that at this time in the morning, or at all if it comes to that." She pulled a hairbrush from her bag and began to work at her flaming locks. "I bet he just wanted to spoil my day. So he witters on for ten minutes about how happy he is, and how wonderful Gina is and how it's going to be a Spring wedding and he's sure I'd get on really well with her, so I said 'You think so?' and he said he was sure of it and I said 'Well think again, but try using your brain not your balls next time' and I hung up. I mean, what does he expect? " She finally paused for breath and sat down facing Josie, who was trying hard to conceal her amusement at Pam's dramatic entrance.

"Good morning Pam. Let me get you a coffee."

"That'd be great. Sorry Jo, I just had to get that off my chest. How are you? "

While Pam was setting out the drawings she had been working on the previous day, Josie told her about Lee's latest escapade, and Pam was suitably sympathetic. She had met Lee a few months ago and had taken to him immediately. She thought he was clever and funny and charming. Unlike a lot of people, she had seen beyond the trappings of his drink problem and connected somehow with the real Lee. Josie loved her for that. When she had finished Pam winked at her.

"What that brother of yours needs is a good woman. Someone to take care of him, apart from you I mean."

Josie laughed. "Did you have anyone particular in mind?" she asked.

Now it was Pam's turn to laugh.

"Well, let me see...who do I know who's unattached at the moment and could use the company of a man with a brain? – Seriously, Jo, why don't you invite us both over to dinner or something? I wouldn't mind helping to sort him out, and he's so...appealing." Josie was about to reply when her mobile phone rang.

"Talk of angels and hear their wings flutter." She said as she looked at the words '*Lee calling*' on the screen of her Nokia and pressed a button to accept the call. Lee sounded sober and quite cheerful. He was ringing because he had woken up and seen the snow. He was so excited about it because he'd always loved snow as a child. He told her he was going outside to clear the path and that he would call her again later. Josie looked across at Pam, and acting on impulse she invited Lee to meet her after work for coffee. Pam was nodding enthusiastically and the arrangement was made to meet at Starbuck's. The conversation ended and the two women giggled at the prospect of a little matchmaking.

The rest of the morning was spent continuing their projects as they listened to a radio station which specialised in playing music from the 'seventies', and singing along to songs from their youth. At half-past twelve Josie rang the Pizza Shop and ordered lunch as Jas had asked her to. He arrived just in time to tip the delivery man. He was looking very pleased with himself as he ushered Josie and Pam into his office and indicated that they should set up the pizzas on the large table usually used for staff meetings.

Jas was bursting with his good news. He had been approached by one of the large greetings card companies. They wanted to start a line of personalised cards and were looking to contract out the design work to a firm who could specialise in that side of the business. Jas's cousin who managed a stationery company had recommended *"Jasuprint"*.

"So, what about it, ladies? Can we pull this off?" He was grinning broadly, his brown eyes twinkling with excitement. "Bespoke Greetings – every card individually designed to the specifications of the customer. Of course they'll have to pay top dollar." His enthusiasm was infectious and Josie felt a rush of excitement at the prospect.

"Of course we can! What a great idea!" she said.

Pam was nodding vigorously, her mouth too full of pizza to speak. Neither of the others had begun eating yet, but now they set about their lunch with a great appetite, talking through their ideas about how the new deal would work. As they were finishing their discussion and clearing away the detritus that remained of their lunch, the phone on Jas's desk rang. He picked up the receiver and after listening for a minute, he handed it to Josie. It was the local hospital, enquiring if she was the next-of-kin to Mr Lee Andrews. Her heart sank and she gripped the edge of the desk as she replied.

"Yes, I'm his sister. What's happened?" she listened in silence for several minutes and then thanked the nurse, said she would be there this evening and replaced the receiver. Pam and Jas had finished clearing the table and were avoiding looking in her direction to give her some privacy while she composed herself. She took a deep breath.

"Well, I suppose I should start composing flexible verses then. No time like the present." She moved towards the door to return to her own workspace, but Jas put a hand on her shoulder to stop her.

"I don't think so, Jo." He said gently. "Not right now."

She turned towards him, a questioning look on her face. His eyes were full of understanding, even though she had never spoken to him about Lee.

"I don't want to pry, but it's obvious your brother is in hospital – you must go to him now. Family is the most important thing in the world and we must never put work before it. You can write verses tomorrow or the next day, but right now you're needed elsewhere, so go!"

Josie was touched by this kindness and she felt her eyes fill with tears as she muttered her thanks. She returned to her office to pick up her coat and bag. On her way out, she passed Jas who was standing at the door of his office; he spoke so softly she could barely hear him.

"Take care Jo, and don't be sad. The tears cloud those beautiful eyes." A little embarrassed by the compliment, Josie nodded and carried on towards the stairs leading down to the car park.

The drive to the hospital was not an easy one. The roads were in a bad way from the snow, and Josie found it difficult to concentrate. Her mind was completely absorbed with worrying about Lee. The nurse had not been specific about how he came to be there. She had said he was in intensive care and that they had found her name and work telephone number on his records from the diabetes clinic. It was fortunate that he had been wearing the silver identity bracelet with details of his name and condition that she had given him for Christmas, as he had no other ID with him and was in no state to answer questions.

When she finally reached the ward, the staff nurse explained that Lee had been brought in by ambulance following a 999 call. He had been involved in some sort of accident as he had cuts and bruises on his forehead. The doctor who had admitted him didn't think the injuries were too serious, but there was obviously some concussion and Lee had not as yet regained full consciousness for longer than a few minutes. During that time, he hadn't been able to furnish them with any information about anything, as he seemed totally confused. Josie provided the background details that were missing from his file, and reluctantly added the fact that he was an alcoholic and that it was entirely possible that drink may have had a part to play in the present situation. She was both surprised and relieved when the nurse told her that blood tests had shown only trace levels of alcohol, and that therefore it was likely that Lee hadn't had a drink for about 24 hours. Further scans and tests would take place tomorrow.

Sitting by Lee's bed, holding his hand and willing him to wake up and talk to her, Josie realised how young he still looked in repose. His rounded features still bore some traces of the long gone childhood.

He was such a beautiful child and everyone loved him. He could make Josie laugh like no-one else could. She was ten years old and confined to bed with tonsillitis. Mum had always insisted that if you were too sick to go to school, then you stayed in bed. It had been a quiet day, reading and sleeping, struggling to swallow her penicillin tablets after breakfast and lunch. By four o'clock she was feeling bored and tearful. The front door opened and closed noisily and she heard the clatter of footsteps racing up the stairs and the "clunk" as a school bag was unceremoniously dumped on the landing. The door burst open and there was Lee like the sun breaking through the clouds. He was laughing and telling her a thousand things at once. He'd made friends with another dog on the way home; (this was a regular occurrence – animals loved him.) He'd asked Sister Mary Patricia to pray for Josie's "Thore Froat" to get better and he had heard several new jokes which spilled out one after the other. Josie laughed so hard it made her cough and Lee held a glass of water for her to drink and patted her back the way Mum did. His cure was more effective than the antibiotics.

Lee stirred and opened his eyes. He blinked in confusion and attempted to sit up but couldn't. Looking at Josie blankly he tried to speak, but couldn't do that either. He took a deep breath and tried again. "Nurse? ...water please." He managed. Josie helped him raise his head from the pillow and held a glass to his lips. She realised that he didn't recognise her and tried not to let it upset her. He was probably in shock she thought. She pressed the buzzer by his bed to let the nurses know he was conscious, but by the time someone came he had drifted off again. The nurse checked his pulse and his temperature and told Josie that he seemed to be stable and that she shouldn't worry.

Half an hour later, he stirred again. This time, he managed a smile of recognition. Josie touched his forehead; it felt hot and clammy.

"Hey Sis, your hand's cold. Are you ok?"

"I should be asking you that." She said. "What happened?" Lee's brow wrinkled as he tried to remember.

"I'm not too sure." He said. "I cleared the snow off the path and then I was going to the cash point. I don't remember much else, apart from a glancing blow."

"A what?"

"A glancing blow to the side of my head. God, it still hurts. I think it was a train." His eyes were starting to glaze over and his speech was slurring. Josie glanced at her watch and realised that she hadn't got much time left if she wanted to keep the peace at home by being there before Rick. She took Lee's hand and squeezed it gently to get his attention.

"I've got to go now, Lee, but I'll be back later."

Lee grinned. "Ah yes. Rotten Rick'll want his tea I expect."

There had never been any love lost between Lee and his brother-in-law. "Go on then, Sis. I'll be OK here 'til you come again."

Josie embraced him and hurried off; stopping only to make sure that the ward sister had her contact details in case there was any change. As she settled into the car and fastened her seat belt, her phone started to ring. The caller's number was not displayed and her first instinct was to ignore the call and see if the caller would leave a message. Curiosity won in the end and she pushed the button to accept the call.

"Jo, it's me." Jas sounded hesitant. "I didn't know if I should call or not. I just wondered if everything was OK."

"I think so, Jas. No-one's quite sure what happened, least of all Lee, but he doesn't seem to be too badly hurt. They're running tests and stuff, so he'll be in for a couple of days."

"I'm glad it's nothing serious. How are you feeling?"

"I'm very tired now, but I'll be fine. It was good of you to call. I'll be in work tomorrow for sure."

"Only if you feel up to it. Take care Jo, 'bye."

Chapter Three

*'The past's another country' – a phrase that I once read
The things we left behind there can seem as good as dead
And yet, I've often wondered how different it would be
If you had never gone away, but stayed to comfort me.*

(From Josie's Journal- Cards for All Occasions)

The next few weeks seemed to fly past. Rick was seldom at home until very late and he had taken to sleeping in the spare room. Susie was busy studying for her A levels and being in love. Lee came out of hospital and managed to stay out of trouble for a while, leaving Josie to enjoy a period of respite from her usual round of worrying. In a strange way, she felt almost redundant at home and only really felt alive when she was working.

Towards Easter the first orders started to arrive for the "bespoke" greetings cards and life at Jasuprint was exciting and busy. Jo and Pam were producing some of their very best work and Jas was drumming up even more business for the firm. He seemed to float around the office with a permanent grin on his face. Success suited him and the two women could not help but notice.

On Maundy Thursday, Jas announced that they would start their Easter break early as he had decided they should all take Friday off, as well as Monday and Tuesday. Pam was delighted. She had recently met a new man at a singles' club and was looking forward to spending some quality time with him over the holiday weekend. She was the first to leave at the end of the day as Mark was meeting her. Josie remained at her desk to add the finishing touches to the last verse of the day. After half an hour she became aware that Jas had entered the office and was standing over her.

"I'm not paying overtime, you know." He said. "Go on home now, Jo. Your family will be missing you."

"I doubt it." Jo blurted out without thinking, and before she knew it a tear rolled down her cheek. She did not really want the office to close for five days, leaving her to spend the holiday weekend largely alone. She took a deep breath and tried to control herself but it was too late. Jas was on his knees turning her swivel chair to face him.

"What's up Jo? Is there anything I can do?" His concern was apparent in the tone of his voice and the softening of his dark brown eyes. Josie wondered why Rick never looked at her like that. Why he neither knew nor cared if she was hurting. The trickle of tears, which she had tried so hard to hold back, became a torrent and as Jas put his arms around her and stroked her back comfortingly, she realised how much she missed being held in someone's arms. The weeping subsided and as she drew back and reached for a tissue, embarrassment took over. Without making eye contact with Jas she dried her eyes and blew her nose.

"I'm sorry," she mumbled, "I don't know what came over me. I hope I haven't stained your shirt." Jas stood up and looked down at the damp spots that were the only remaining traces of their embrace.

"I'll survive." He laughed gently. "The question is, will you?" Josie turned towards him sheepishly and managed a half-smile.

"I suppose so," she said. "Everyone needs a good bout of self-pity from time to time. I should go home and get on with it." She turned off her computer and rose to leave. Jas helped her into her coat and told her to have a good weekend. As she headed for the stairs, she heard him locking the doors as he prepared to go home.

Driving home, Josie felt foolish for having let go of her emotions like that. What must he think of her? He was so kind and his arms had felt so warm and strong when he held her. She could still smell his after-shave; a subtle, spicy fragrance that suited him so well. She remembered feeling his heartbeat as she had sobbed against his chest. She sighed as she parked the car in front of the house and realised there was no sign of life. It was a quarter to six, and she assumed that Susie had gone to Peter's. She would be spending the evening alone again.

Sitting in the kitchen with a cup of tea in front of her she decided to phone Lee. She hadn't heard from him for a couple of days and she felt she needed to hear the sound of his voice. He answered immediately and he sounded happy and sober. They chatted inconsequentially for a few minutes, just long enough for Josie to realise that Lee was not really listening to her. She was about to ask him if anything was wrong when she heard sounds in the background which told her he was not alone.

"Sorry, Lee. Have you got company? I didn't think." She could almost hear him grinning mischievously as he replied.

"Nothing gets past you does it, Sis? I'll tell you what – I'll call you tomorrow and fill you in, OK?"

"OK." She said, but Lee had already hung up. She made herself some toast and took it into the sitting room with the now cold cup of tea. She decided that she would spend the evening watching whatever drivel she could find on the TV. She also decided that she would definitely not spend any more time thinking about "Jasuprint". The latter proved to be the more difficult task as her mind kept returning to the moments when Jas had held her, and how good it had felt. She flicked through the channels and eventually settled on a documentary about an author she had never heard of. She lay back on the sofa and soon drifted off to sleep.

Rick phoned at half-past seven to say that he would be away overnight on a business trip. Still drowsy from her nap, Josie thought she heard the sound of laughter and music in the background of their short conversation. Angry, but afraid to let it show too much, she asked what time he expected to be back the next day. He muttered something about calling in the morning and hung up quickly. Returning to the sofa she picked up her mobile and called Susie. The call went straight to voicemail, so Susie had either turned her phone off or the battery was dead again. It seemed that everyone had something better to do tonight than Josie did. The mobile vibrated to announce the arrival of a text message. She opened it and read:

"ON PETE'S MOB. MY BATT'S DIED.
STAYING OVER 2NITE. C U 2MORO.
LV SUS X"

Josie threw the mobile down beside her with a sigh of frustration. She didn't want to be alone all night. After Rick's call she had wanted to talk to her daughter and maybe seek reassurance from her, but it obviously wasn't meant to happen. She would have to make do with her own company, and worst of all her own thoughts. Oh well, when all else failed, there was always a bath and an early night. Halfway up to the bathroom she heard the buzz of her message tone again. She was tempted to leave it until later, but curiosity got the better of her and she turned back. It was from a number she didn't recognise.

"HOPE YOU'RE OK NOW. THIS IS MY
NEW NUMBER. CALL IF YOU
NEED ANYTHING. JAS"

She read the message several times, once again astonished at Jas's kindness. She decided to call him to say thanks. It would be nice to talk to someone for a few minutes. It took a little while to psych herself up, but finally she dialled the number. He answered almost immediately.

"Hello Jo. I was hoping you'd call" Josie was taken aback.

"How did you know?"

"Caller display. You're in my memory, er, that is your number's in the memory of my phone." They both laughed.

"Yes of course" said Jo "I wasn't thinking."

"Are you ok? I was concerned."

"I'm fine now. I just called to say thanks."

"So are you having a nice evening?" Josie felt herself becoming a little emotional. She didn't want to sound pathetic so she took a deep breath and said that she was enjoying a quiet evening alone. They chatted for a few minutes longer, mainly about work. Finally, Jas said,

"Jo, I hope you regard me as a friend as well as a colleague. If you need any help, or even just a chat. I'm here, you know."

Josie felt more cheerful now, and seriously hungry. She decided to treat herself and ordered a takeaway from her favourite Indian restaurant. Half an hour later she was sitting on the floor eating Chicken Tikka Masala and pilau rice out of the cartons and watching a topical comedy show on the TV, thinking that her night alone might be quite pleasant after all. There would be no washing-up except for the fork she was using and her coffee mug, and she had complete control of the TV remote for a change. All thoughts of an early night had now left her as she began scrolling through the channels to find out what her choices were. Then the phone rang.

Susie was sobbing and almost incoherent. Josie managed to fathom that she and Peter had argued and Susie had set off for home only to realise that she had left her bus pass at Peter's. She had no cash with her and her phone battery was dead so she was in a call box and had reversed the charges to call her mother. Josie soothed her and took down the details of her whereabouts, promising that she would pick her up and warning her to stay where she was, preferably inside the call box. As Josie hung up and grabbed her car keys and purse she wondered if life would ever be simple.

*

It is never easy to deal with someone who believes their heart has been broken, but when that someone is your own child it is almost impossible. Through the night and into the small hours of Good Friday morning Josie comforted her daughter and raged inwardly against the young man who had hurt her so badly. Susie wept an ocean of tears as she told how she had found out that the love of her life was seeing someone else. Her beautiful young face was pale and her eyes were swollen and red-rimmed as she sobbed out her anguish. Josie held her and wept with her, quite unable to explain to her daughter why she sympathised so completely.

"Perhaps you're mistaken." She said. "Things aren't always what they seem." Susie looked up at her.

"No, Mum. There's no mistake. He's admitted it."

"How could he do this to you? He's a worthless scumbag! He'd better hope he never runs into me again, or your dad for that matter." Susie was sobbing again.

"No, Mum. Please don't tell Dad yet. I couldn't bear it if he got into one of his rages with Peter. I don't want you to hate him; I can't even hate him myself."

Her confusion was even harder to bear than her distress. Josie hugged her until the tears subsided, and as dawn was breaking she led her upstairs and tucked her into bed as if she was a little girl again, stroking her daughter's hair until she fell into an exhausted sleep. Leaving the room quietly, Josie realised that she was now beyond sleep, having gone way past tiredness. The sun was breaking through with the promise of a warm spring day ahead, so she showered and dressed and took a cup of coffee and a bowl of cereal out into the garden. For some time she sat gazing into the distance, occasionally noticing little tasks that would have to be attended to soon. The lawn needed mowing and there would be some weeding to do.

She thought about Rick and her heart felt heavy. The cold spell between them had been the longest ever. They weren't arguing, so that was something, but they weren't communicating either. Every effort she made was rebuffed or ignored. They were like strangers, being uncomfortably polite to each other. She would have liked to talk to him about Susie, but she had promised not to, and in any case, he would only fly into a rage and they could all do without that. At least he hadn't lost his temper with either his wife or his daughter for quite a few weeks now.

"Whoever she is, she's keeping him happy." Josie said to herself as she got up and took her breakfast things back inside. She busied herself with tidying up and sorting out the laundry. Then she sat at the kitchen table to make a shopping list. She decided she would ask Susie to go shopping with her and let her choose some of her favourite treats. She would also call round to see Lee and ask him over for Sunday lunch.

Feeling more at ease now that she had made some plans she picked up the novel Pam had lent her the day before and settled on the sofa to read for an hour before waking Susie. It was a romance, of the type her mother had always referred to as a "penny dreadful". The "blurb" on the back described it as a *torrid tale of forbidden love set against the background of the industrial Midlands in the 1960s"* Josie laughed to herself, thinking that there had surely been no such thing as "forbidden love" in that golden decade. She started to read and was soon so engrossed in the story that she lost all track of time. It was almost two hours later when she heard the front door bell and put the book down.

She opened the door and for a moment was unable to catch her breath. She stared in disbelief at the man standing on the path. He was a lot older than when she had last seen him, but the blue eyes still sparkled with mischief. He looked rather shabby in an overcoat that had seen better days and scuffed brown shoes. He was holding a rucksack by one strap, the other having broken. He grinned at her and she finally found her voice.

"Dad? What are you doing here? Where have you been?"

"That's a fine greeting!" he said "Don't I get a hug anymore?" He held out his arms and Josie rushed into them, the strength of her joy taking all her questions away for the time being.

It was her wedding day, 20 years ago. The day had been pleasant enough although tinged with sadness; Josie's mother Annie had died suddenly a month before the big day and Josie, Lee and her father were still grieving. They had decided not to cancel the wedding. Annie had been looking forward to it so much and they were all sure she would have wanted it to go ahead as planned. The service and the formalities were over; Josie had changed out of her bridal gown and into her "going away outfit", a dark green trouser suit with a cream silk blouse that suited her dark colouring and trim figure. They were flying to Paris for their honeymoon.

She went into the hall to say goodbye to the guests and realised that her father had left, without saying a word. Believing that the occasion may have been too emotional for him, she let it pass, but on her return from Paris, she discovered that the home she had grown up in was up for sale and her father had gone away without leaving a forwarding address.

Lee knew nothing about it either, and since then neither of them had heard a word from him. They tried tracing him, but if someone really does not want to be found even the most determined searcher will not find them. Arrangements had evidently been made for the proceeds from the sale of the family home to be invested, and the accountants handling the investments remained silent about the whereabouts of their client; only willing to confirm that he was alive and well.

Twenty years on, here he was at last, standing on her doorstep as if he'd never been away. Josie pulled away from the embrace, her tears stinging her eyes as the anger and hurt surfaced at last.

"How could you do it Dad? How could you disappear like that and leave us?"

"Do you think we should have that conversation out here, love? Aren't you going to invite me in?" He also seemed very close to tears as Josie led him into the house and made a pot of tea. They sat at the kitchen table in silence for a few minutes. Finally, the old man started to speak.

"I ran away, Jo. It's as simple as that. At first, I didn't mean to stay away for so long; just a few months maybe, to get over losing your mum. I meant to come back for Christmas that first year. I tried to call Lee but he'd moved again, and when I called here I realised I wasn't going to be well-received and that I'd lost you too." He was weeping openly now.

"You called here? When?" Josie was stunned.

"That Christmas Eve, you were out shopping. Rick said you wouldn't want to see me; that I'd abandoned you and you didn't need me now that you had him. He sent me away and said that I shouldn't bother to call again."

Josie was speechless. This was something new to her. She reached across the table and grasped her father's hand. Their eyes met and a look of sudden understanding passed between them. Josie did not have to explain that she had never been told of his visit. When she had recovered her composure a little, she smiled and changed the subject.

"You have a granddaughter." She announced. The old man grinned mischievously.

"I know." He said "Susan, known as Susie. A beautiful and charming young lady."

Now Josie was mystified. She opened her mouth to voice the question when she heard the unmistakeable sound of her daughter coming downstairs.

Susie still looked pale and drained but as she entered the kitchen, her face lit up. "Granddad! You came after all!" she exclaimed as she rushed to hug him.

"How could I not, sweetheart?" he replied rising to greet her. Josie was dumbfounded. She tried to speak but words failed her completely as she looked from one to the other. It felt like a dream of some kind and she was sure she would wake up at any moment. Finally she found her voice.

"Will one of you please tell me what's happening here? How do you two know each other?"

Susie and her grandfather exchanged a glance and replied in unison."The library."

They both laughed and Susie went on to explain.

They had met in the City library when she was studying for her mock exams before Christmas. Susie had a coughing fit and couldn't draw breath. The old man who was sitting at a table reading a newspaper came to her rescue. He handed her a brown paper bag and told her to blow into it until her breathing settled down again. Afterwards he asked the librarian to get her a glass of water. She thanked him and took his advice that perhaps it was time to call it a day and go home for a rest. She saw him in the library several times after that, and they always greeted one another. It wasn't until the last day of term when her exams were over that they really got into conversation and discovered their connection.

Susie had been giving out Christmas cards to her classmates at college when she suddenly thought about the old man from the library. She wondered if he had anyone to send him a card, as he was always alone. On impulse, she took a spare card from the box in her bag and after a few moments of thought, she wrote: "Season's Greetings to the Good Samaritan" she signed it "Susan (Susie) Anson." On her way home from college she called into the library, and sure enough, he was sitting in his usual spot. As she

approached his table, he stood up and smiled at her. Feeling
a little embarrassed she reached into her bag and pulled out
the envelope. As she handed it to him, he chuckled, pulling
an envelope out of his pocket and handing it to her.

"What is it they say about great minds?" he said. Susie
opened her card first. It was signed:

"Kind Regards and best wishes, Joe Andrews." She
thanked him and remarked on the coincidence that Andrews
was her mother's maiden name. Then Joe opened his card,
and looking at her strangely, he asked her to sit down.

"Susie, this is going to sound very odd, but I have a
daughter whose married name is Anson." Susie was
unnerved. She had been brought up with all the usual
warnings about strangers. She hadn't minded passing the
time of day with Joe in the library, but now he seemed to be
acting as if they might be related and she was worried. He
read her concern in her face and was quick to reassure her.

"Don't look so worried. I'm not some scheming old
pervert. It's taken me by surprise that you should have the
same surname as my daughter, that's all. It's surely just a
coincidence. Let's say no more about it." Susie was only too
happy to agree. She left the library quickly and went straight
home, deciding not to tell anyone about her encounter.

In January, she called into the library to return some
books and Joe was there as usual. She tried to avoid meeting
his eyes, but he had been waiting for her and he came over
as she stood at the desk. Without saying a word, he placed a
photograph in front of her. She gasped as she recognised it.
Her mother had a copy of the same one at home. It was Josie
on her First Communion Day, aged seven. She handed her
books to the librarian and followed Joe back to the table.
She looked again at the photograph of her mother in her
white lace dress and veil, and then looked up at Joe waiting
for him to say something.

"She was dressed like that the last time I saw her too."
He said. "Only that time was her wedding day." Now Susie

knew he was speaking the truth. Josie had once told her that she hadn't seen her father since the wedding and that she didn't know where he was. It had been a cause of sadness in her life and Susie hadn't questioned her about it, not wishing to cause any further distress.

Joe looked fondly at his granddaughter as she paused to assess Josie's reaction. He decided it was his turn to speak.

"We met up a few more times and Susie kept telling me she was sure you'd want to see me, but I took some convincing. I hope I've done the right thing. I'd hate to hurt you again." Josie rose from her chair and reached out to embrace both Susie and Joe.

Chapter Four

The gap grows ever wider
The ice is colder yet
And though I keep on trying
It gets harder to forget

(From Josie's journal – Cards for all Occasions)

It was late afternoon when Rick finally put in an appearance. He was wearing a new shirt and carrying a Burton's bag containing the one he had worn yesterday. Josie guessed he had bought new underwear too. His night away from home had been unplanned this time. He was far from pleased to realise that they had company, and even more disgruntled by the fact that his wife and daughter were so obviously enjoying listening to Joe's tales of his adventures over the last twenty years. He grunted a greeting of sorts and went straight into the kitchen where he rattled around noisily. Josie looked at the others and then got up and followed him, closing the door behind her.

"What's he doing here?" Rick asked angrily. "He ignores you for 20 years and then shows up out of the blue. You should have told him piss off." Josie stared at him for a moment and then, very quietly she said

"Like you did the last time you saw him? I don't think so Rick. He's my dad and I've invited him to spend the weekend with us. Well, with Susie and me anyway because we don't know what your plans are yet, do we?"

Rick's face was a picture of confusion. Josie had never spoken to him quite that way before. She was daring to question him and at the same time defying him.

"I don't want that man in my house." He said through gritted teeth. Josie now did the unthinkable and raised her voice.

"Well I want him in *our* house, and so does *our* daughter. So if you want him to leave, then you go and tell him now, in front of Susie, and maybe you can explain to all of us what your problem is." Shaking, she turned and left the kitchen, leaving Rick speechless.

Susie and Joe had heard the last part of the conversation and as Josie walked back into the living room, they silently applauded her with big grins on their faces. A few minutes later Rick came in with a cup of coffee and sat down. He was trying very hard to act as if nothing had happened. He realised that he was outnumbered here, and he needed to regain control. If he was to be lumbered with his father-in-law, then it must appear that he agreed to it. He forced a smile at the old man.

"Well Joe. It's been a long time hasn't it? It's a pity I didn't know you were coming; I'd have arranged to be around so we could catch up." Josie caught the look on Rick's face and guessed what was coming next. "As it is, I have to go away for the weekend; until Tuesday actually, so I expect you'll be gone by then." It was a statement not a question. Susie shot a glance at her mother, and realised that this weekend trip had come as a shock to her.

"Oh Dad," she said, "It's Easter. You surely can't have to work over the holiday?" Rick almost softened as he looked at her. He loved his daughter in his own way, but she was part of this defiance too and he would not encourage her to side with her mother against him.

"Sorry, sweetheart." He sighed, almost convincingly. "Work is work. You'll understand better when you're older." This last remark was calculated to irritate her by reminding her that she would always be a child in his eyes.

Rick had scored his points and he switched on the TV for the evening news, putting an end to any further discussion, as both Susie and Josie knew that it was not wise to talk during the news.

Susie cooked a prawn risotto for dinner. She was a good cook, and the meal looked and smelt wonderful. As they were about to start eating, Rick's mobile phone rang and he excused himself and left the room to take the call. Joe tasted his dinner and patted Susie's hand.

"This is great, love. Your grandmother would have loved it. She was very fond of seafood. She was a fantastic cook wasn't she, little Jo?" Josie laughed at his use of the nickname from her childhood. Her mother had used it all the time to avoid confusion between Joe and Josephine.

"I love it too," Susie replied "and we had to have something fishy today because we don't eat meat on Good Friday." Joe looked at his daughter with a curious expression on his face.

"Is it just old habits, or do you still practise?" he asked. "So many people don't bother nowadays."

"I've never stopped, Dad. Susie and I still go to St. Jude's every Sunday, although I think she only comes to please me. Rick gave up years ago."

"He and I have something in common then. I'm afraid I lost a lot of my faith when your mother died." Josie was about to reply when Rick returned. He took his place and tasted his food. It was cold by now and he pulled a face as he pushed the plate away. Joe offered him a glass of wine, which he refused, saying that he would be driving shortly.

"Where will you be if we need to get in touch?" asked Josie, knowing that she was unlikely to get a straight answer. Rick scowled, although he must have expected the question.

"In meetings." He said. "You can always leave a message on my mobile, but I can't see that you'll need me for anything. Now, if you'll excuse me," he rose abruptly from the table. "I have to pack." With that, he went quickly upstairs, and ten minutes later, he reappeared as they were clearing the table. He was casually dressed in jeans and a sweatshirt and carried a small holdall. Josie was certain that this would not contain one of his business suits. Shaking hands with Joe and kissing his daughter's cheek, he left the house without saying anything to Josie. She sighed and carried the dishes through to the kitchen with distinctly mixed feelings.

Chapter Five

What would I do if I were alone?
How would I cope, here on my own?
Your friendship is now my consolation
Guiding me through my desperation

(From Josie's Journal – Cards for all Occasions)

The weekend had been fun and Josie felt relaxed and happy as she drove to work on Wednesday. She and Joe had spent hours catching up on the missing years. She had been fascinated to hear that he had given up his lucrative career in advertising to go travelling. He had visited most of the countries in Europe, working in bars and cafés when he needed ready money. He had not touched his investments, and had even managed to save. Five years ago, he had bought a small cottage in Normandy, and this was now his home.

He had returned to England in December to meet with his accountant and had decided to stick around for a few weeks. Then he had met Susie and this had kept him here longer. He was going back to France tomorrow, reconciled with Josie and Lee, and having elicited promises that they would visit him soon.

Josie was happy about Lee too. He had come over for lunch on Sunday and he seemed fitter than she had seen him in a long time. He was sober and refused the offer of a drink, saying that he had met someone special and he was trying to "clean up his act".

Arriving at work, Josie was surprised to find that Jas was already there. She put her head around the door of his office and asked if he wanted coffee. He raised his eyes from his paperwork and smiled.

"Well, aren't you an angel? I was just thinking I needed some caffeine." He got up from his desk and following her through to her office. Over coffee, she told him about her father and the weekend, omitting any reference to Rick. She did not know why, but she was reluctant to let Jas know how unhappy Rick was making her at present.

At nine o'clock Pam arrived and the day took on its usual comfortable format. Jas presented them with a list of clients who wished to avail themselves of the custom greetings cards service, and Josie spent the morning making phone calls to obtain specific details of their requirements. She prided herself on making sure every one of her verses was personal, and although she occasionally used certain phrases or lines more than once, no two were identical. She had become quite adept at including names and anecdotes supplied by the clients so that the recipient knew that a lot of thought had gone into the card. Jas had received several letters of thanks and many referrals because of this.

At lunchtime, she went out to meet Lee. He was bringing his girlfriend along and Josie was excited at the prospect of meeting the cause of her brother's reform. She chose a table in the window of the café where they were to meet, and ordered a glass of orange juice while she waited. She did not worry too much when Lee did not show up on time. Punctuality had never been his strong point, and a new love interest could make anyone a little forgetful she imagined. After fifteen minutes, she ordered a sandwich. After all, she would have to go back to work soon, so she could not wait until they arrived to eat.

Her sandwich eaten, though not really tasted, she glanced at her watch and realised it was time to go back to work. She was cross, but still not really worried. Lee had stood her up before; it was just that he often lost track of time. She would call him later and arrange to meet another day.

Pam was already back at her workstation and deeply involved in a sketch she was preparing for a retirement card they were working on. She looked up when Josie came in.

"Nice lunch?" she asked, "What's she like – the sister-in-law?" Josie laughed and told her that she still didn't know. She switched on her computer and prepared to spend the afternoon in creative mode.

For a change, the two women worked in silence, each deep in concentration on her own task. The time passed quickly and Josie was surprised when her mobile rang and she realised it was already four o'clock. She glanced at the display screen and saw that it was Lee's number.

"Where were you at lunchtime?" she said without preamble. It was not Lee who answered, but a strange female voice.

"Is that Jo, Lee's sister?" the voice was shaky and slightly indistinct. "Something's wrong. I can't wake him up."

"Who is this? What's happened?" Josie was on her feet now, reaching for her bag and car keys. "Are you at the flat?"

"It's Maggie, Lee's, er, friend. We were supposed to meet you today but we fell asleep and now I can't wake him. Can you come now, please?" Her speech was punctuated by sobs.

"Are you at Lee's place?" Josie asked again, by now halfway out of the door.

"Yes, yes." Maggie was almost screaming. "Are you coming? I don't know what to do!"

"I'll be there in ten minutes. Call an ambulance. If it gets there before I do call me and let me know where they take him." Josie was scared now too. She did not like the sound of this at all. She ended the call and shoved her phone into her pocket racing for the staircase, unaware that Jas was standing outside his office watching her go.

He caught up with her as she fumbled with the key, her hands shaking, and tears blurring her vision. Taking the keys from her, he said.

"It's OK Jo. I'll drive; just tell me where we're going."

He helped her into the passenger seat and fastened the seat belt around her then quickly went round and got into the driving seat. Josie gave him the address and he nodded to say that he knew where it was, then the engine roared into life and they sped away towards Lee's, with Josie explaining the crisis on the way.

The door to the flat was standing open when they arrived so they walked straight in. There was no sign of Maggie or Lee. Josie called out, but got no response.

"The ambulance must have been already," said Jas, putting an arm around her shoulders. "They'll be on their way to the hospital I expect." Josie leaned against him, grateful of the company and support.

"She was supposed to call me, to say where they were taking him. What do I do now?" She felt helpless. There were at least four emergency units in the city and she could not think straight. Jas stroked her arm to calm her down.

"You call her." He said gently, and Josie realised that this was the obvious thing to do. She gave him a tearful smile and took out her phone. She dialled Lee's mobile number, but as it connected, she heard it ringing out from the bedroom. Maggie had not taken it with her. Once again, Jas was calm and logical.

"Perhaps she has her own phone?" He suggested. "Surely Lee will have her number saved in his?" They went into the bedroom and picked up the handset, which was lying on the floor. Jo scrolled through to the contacts page, but there was no Maggie listed. The only recent addition had been the two contact numbers Joe had given them on Sunday. She put the phone down and looked around her. The room was a mess. The duvet and sheet lay in a heap on the floor exposing the mattress, and to her alarm, Josie noticed a syringe on the bedside table. It was not one of Lee's insulin syringes and she feared the worst. Unable to think logically, she had to do something, so she picked up the sheet and started to make the bed. She had forgotten that she was not

40

alone and when Jas spoke after a few minutes she was startled out of her reverie.

"Sorry," she said. "I'm afraid I didn't hear you."

"I don't want to worry you even more," His voice was tense. "But she didn't call an ambulance; at least not with this phone." He had been checking the call log and the last call had been to Josie. She slumped onto the bed feeling totally helpless. She was sobbing quietly. Jas looked down at her for a moment and then left the room, returning with a strong cup of coffee that he held for her to sip. When she had calmed down a little, Jas took out his own mobile and made a call. Josie could not understand what he was saying, and it took her a minute to realise that he was speaking in Punjabi. In the time she had known him, it had never occurred to her before that English was not his first and only language. She looked at him quizzically as he ended the call, but he held up his hand to indicate that he was not ready to explain yet as he quickly dialled another number. He spoke in English this time, to Pam. He told her that something had come up and that neither he nor Jo would be back in the office today. She should lock up and go home and they would see her tomorrow. Pam had a lot of questions to ask which Jas fended off by saying he was expecting a call and would have to go. Then he ended the call and smiled at Josie.

"I called my sister, Suki. She's a doctor and she's ringing all the A and E units to see if your brother's been admitted anywhere. She'll call me as soon as she has any news. Now let me help you finish tidying up. Being busy will make you feel better while we wait."

The waiting seemed endless, despite the fact that they were occupied. Together they finished making the bed, and then Jas tackled some washing-up in the kitchen while Josie loaded the washing machine with a pile of clothes she found on the bathroom floor. They were all Lee's, so she guessed that Maggie hadn't been in the habit of staying here on a regular basis.

The living room was tidy except for the cluttered coffee table in front of the sofa. Josie folded the newspaper that was spread out there and emptied the ashtray. A pack of Marlboro and a disposable lighter lay beside it and without thinking Josie took out a cigarette and lit it. Jas looked at her in amazement.

"I didn't know you smoked." He said. Jo spluttered as the smoke hit her lungs, and then replied hoarsely.

"I don't, at least I haven't for the last five years, but I just needed this one. I'm sorry." She reached for the ashtray to stub it out, but he stopped her.

"Don't apologise. Smoke it if it helps. We all need our own props. Personally, I prefer to have a drink. I don't suppose your brother has any vodka?"

"Only in his bloodstream, I suspect, but we can look." said Jo and suddenly they were both laughing.

They found a bottle containing two shots of cheap brandy in the kitchen, which they shared, and then the call came through. Suki had located Lee but the news was not good. He had been taken to the hospital and left in the reception area by two men who had left without giving an explanation. He was comatose and pending the outcome of tests it looked like an accidental overdose of what the doctors described as recreational drugs.

Suki said the hospital had identified him because he had a note pinned to his tee shirt with his name and address on it. Obviously, the people who had deposited him there wanted to be helpful but remain anonymous.

Without the need for further discussion, Josie and Jas locked up the flat and headed for the hospital.

Chapter Six

The light of my life is fading away
Is God even listening to me, as I pray?

(From Josie's Journal —Cards for all Occasions)

While Jas was driving, Josie phoned Susie and explained the situation, asking her to contact Joe and let him know. As an afterthought, she added:

"If your Dad shows up you can tell him too. I don't know how long I'll be. I'm not leaving until I know what's going on."

Susie agreed to pass on the messages and said that she would stay at home until Rick arrived. They both knew that he would not take kindly to coming home to an empty house.

The hospital was busy as usual and Josie was kept waiting for half an hour before she could get any information about Lee. Jas stayed with her and fetched coffee from the vending machine for both of them. There was little conversation between them, but the silence was not uncomfortable. Jas realised that she was far too worried to make small talk, but when she suggested he should leave and go home he simply shook his head.

"It's OK, Jo. I'm not in any hurry. I don't think you should be alone right now."

"Thanks." she said, weakly. "I expect Dad will be here soon if Susie was able to get through to him."

Finally, she heard the receptionist call out her name, and she was introduced to the doctor who had just been examining Lee. As she was following him into an office at the side of the main reception, her father arrived and joined them. He hugged her and they sat down as the doctor opened a thick file of case notes with Lee's name on the front.

An hour later, having spent a few minutes with Lee, who was still unconscious, Joe and Josie were preparing to leave. They had a lot to discuss and needed to get away from the hospital to do it. As they walked back through the lobby, the receptionist handed Josie an envelope containing her car keys and a slip of paper bearing the words:

"Call me. I'll be thinking about you- Jas"

She folded the note carefully and put it into her bag then tucked her arm through Joe's as they headed for the car park. She called Susie and who told her that Rick still had not returned. She breathed a sigh of relief and ushered Joe into the car.

Back at home, Susie had made sandwiches and a fresh pot of coffee, then sensing that they needed some space she withdrew to her bedroom. There was a long silence and finally Josie said:

"So what should we do Dad?" Her father stared into his cup and said nothing. "You heard what the doctor said. If he comes out of this, there's a good chance Lee could be seriously brain-damaged."

"And if he doesn't come out of it? What happens then Jo?" His voice was shaking. "Are we going to let him vegetate, hooked up to those machines forever? That's not Lee. That's just the husk of what he used to be." The old man was crying now. "We have to do what's right for him."

"How do we know what that is? I mean, he could be fine. He could just wake up with no damage, couldn't he?" Josie was desperately trying to believe this was true.

"Please don't do this to yourself, little Jo. You know that's not likely to happen. You have to tell them that if his heart or breathing stops they should let him go in peace."

Josie could see the logic of her father's words, but they went against everything she believed and felt in her heart. This was not just a hypothetical case. This was her beloved brother they were discussing. She sobbed and held her father's hand across the table.

"You'll be with me won't you?" she asked, but the old man shook his head.

"I'm going back tomorrow as planned, I'm afraid. I haven't the stomach for this."

Josie stared at him in amazement.

"You can't mean that? You waltz back into my life after all these years and then tell me that you can't stick around for an extra day when I really need you."

Joe was unable to raise his eyes to meet hers.

"I'm sorry, truly I am, but I can't wait around to watch my son die or wake up a vegetable."

"No, but I have to watch it happen to my brother. You're a coward Dad, and you're running away again."

Joe didn't reply. Josie was on her feet now and marching towards the front door. She held it open.

"Well, you'd better go and pack your things. I'll manage without you as I've had to for the last 20 years."

Joe rose from the table, unable to say anything. As he reached the front door, Susie appeared at the top of the stairs.

"Going so soon Granddad?" she asked, bounding down the stairs to hug him. "When will you be back?"

Joe held her tightly saying: "I don't know love, but you could always come to visit me you know."

"I'd like that." She said, looking to her mother for approval and not understanding why Josie simply shrugged and went back into the kitchen, closing the door behind her.

Joe left and Susie turned towards the kitchen where she could hear her mother clattering pots and pans as she started to prepare the evening meal. She went in to offer help, sensing that something was wrong, but before she could say anything the phone rang and Josie rushed to answer it. To her astonishment, it was Rick telling her that he would be home in half an hour. He said she should get ready because they would be eating out, just the two of them. She really did not feel up to it, but she was anxious as ever not to upset him so she agreed. She hung up and turned towards Susie.

"Can you fend for yourself this evening? Dad and I are going out." She said. Susie's face was a picture of confusion.

"What? Together?" she asked, and then laughed. "I mean that's great! I'll sort myself out. You enjoy yourselves."

*

Josie chose her outfit with great care. She had no idea what this was all about, but if Rick wanted to take her out it must mean that there was hope for their relationship. It was a mild evening, so she opted for a blue cotton skirt and a white blouse. As an afterthought, she picked up a blue pashmina that almost matched the skirt and draped it loosely around her shoulders. Standing before the full-length mirror, she was quite pleased with the effect. She made up her eyes, but only lightly, as Rick didn't like to see her looking "tarty" as he put it. When she was ready, she called Susie and asked her opinion.

"Mum, you look lovely. I hope Dad appreciates it!" she said and she picked up a perfume bottle and sprayed the light floral scent on her mother's neck, just as they heard Rick opening the front door.

They dined at a Greek restaurant, which had been one of their favourite haunts early in their marriage. The food was still excellent and Rick persuaded Josie to have a half-bottle of red wine, even though he was not drinking himself because he was driving. He complimented the way she looked and even managed to show an interest when she told him of the day's events with Lee, and her father's departure. He took her hand across the table and said:

"Well, I'll be here to help you. Do you want me to come to the hospital tomorrow evening? I'd be moral support for you." Josie's gratitude overwhelmed her and in an instant, it was as if she had forgotten all her recent hurt and anguish.

"Thank you, Rick. I'd be really glad of your support." Rick noticed that her eyes were misting over with tears so squeezing her hand gently he said:

"Why don't we skip dessert and go home? You look exhausted, darling." Josie sighed with contentment. It was a long time since he'd called her that.

Back at home, they found a note from Susie saying she had gone to bed early and hoped they had had a good time. Rick made coffee while Josie stretched out on the sofa. She was feeling a little nervous, wondering how long this new Rick was going to be around, and where it was all leading. When he brought the steaming mugs through from the kitchen, he placed them on the coffee table and looked down at her thoughtfully.

"Here, let me make you more comfortable." He said, kneeling down and removing her shoes. He started to rub her feet gently and then kissed her toes one at a time. She began to relax a little. The wine from earlier was still coursing through her veins and suddenly she wanted nothing more than to feel Rick's arms around her. Sensing this, Rick stood up and taking her hand led her up to their bedroom; a room he had not slept in for months.

He held her face between his hands and the kiss that followed reminded her of the first kiss they had ever shared – slow and tentative at first and then building in intensity and desire. She allowed herself to be steered towards the bed, excited now, but knowing of old that she must not let it show. One attempt at taking the initiative on her part and the mood would be broken. He would tell her when she should respond and how. She lay down and watched as he undressed, longing to touch him, but knowing she must wait. Not for too long though, as his arousal was very noticeable.

Later, the lovemaking over, Rick rolled away from her and fell asleep instantly. Josie lay awake and listened to him breathing for a long time. Her emotions were confused. Part of her was thrilled that Rick had come back to her tonight, at a time when she most needed to be loved, but there was also the disappointment, which she scarcely dared to admit, even to herself. She had wanted him so much tonight, had been revelling in the closeness that had been lacking for so long, but as she had approached her climax Rick reached his and that was all that mattered. He would never think to wait for her; and then he had fallen asleep. Had it always been like this? In her frustration, she thought that it had. Still, at least he hadn't hurt her tonight and he was back in their bed. She smiled to herself as she remembered how good it had felt to be the object of his desire again. Finally, she drifted off to sleep.

She stood on a balcony, looking out across a moonlit sea. It was a warm but breezy night and the white silk gown she was wearing fluttered against her skin. It felt good, and she felt good as she inhaled the warm air. She did not hear him come outside to join her, but she sensed his presence as he stood behind her and she closed her eyes as he placed his hands on her shoulders and turned her around. He touched her forehead with his lips and whispered:

"Look at me, Jo. Let me see your beautiful eyes." But she could not, or would not open her eyes. She leaned against him as he enfolded her in his arms and sighed.

"I can't look at you, not this way. If I don't see you it won't be wrong, and I don't want it to be wrong." He seemed to understand and with her eyes still closed, she allowed herself to be led inside. The coupling was a meeting of minds and hearts as well as bodies. It was slow and tender; thoughtful and gentle followed by warm and soft embraces until she fell asleep, her head resting on his shoulder and his arms wrapped around her.

She awoke with a start. Rick was snoring away beside her. She blushed as she remembered her dream and was glad that she hadn't been restless enough to disturb him. She wondered who her dream partner had been, for it certainly hadn't been Rick. She checked the time and then settled down to sleep again, this time dreamlessly.

48

Chapter Seven

Is this for real, or is it a mask?
Have you come back to me? I have to ask
I have to know if I can depend
On your love and support when I most need a friend.

(From Josie's Journal – Cards for all Occasions)

The alarm clock woke her at six-thirty. She was alone in the bedroom but she could smell bacon and coffee from downstairs. She guessed that Susie was up early for a change, and then she remembered Rick. She hurried downstairs and there he was, in the kitchen preparing breakfast. In the cold light of day, Josie realised that he looked stressed and tired. She also realised that she had not asked him what had brought about his change of attitude. She thought of asking him now, but quickly decided that perhaps it was better not to know. She would live for the moment and enjoy it while it lasted. She sat down and smiled as he placed a heaped plateful of bacon and eggs in front of her. He was grinning like a little boy and she hadn't the heart to tell him that she almost never ate fried food these days; that was something else that could wait. He was trying so hard. She looked up as he spoke.

"I'll be home around four-thirty so we can go to see Lee."

"That's great." She said. "I'll call the hospital this morning and see how things are."

Rick was shrugging himself into his suit jacket as he bent down to kiss the top of her head.

"I've got to go, love. I'll call you later." He picked up his car keys and left.

Josie's head was reeling with unanswered questions, which she tried to push out of her mind. She left her breakfast largely untouched and finished her coffee, before going upstairs to shower and dress for work.

As she was preparing to leave the house, Susie put in an appearance. She looked so young this morning with her tousled hair and wearing pyjamas with a teddy bear design. She also seemed to be very tired, as if she hadn't slept well.

"Are you OK, love?" Josie asked, "You don't look well." Susie shook her head slowly.

"I'll get over it," she said. "Don't worry about me; you've got enough problems of your own. See you later." She helped herself to a glass of water and went back to bed.

Jas was already in the office when Jo arrived. He had managed to fathom out how the coffee maker worked and he handed her a cup as she sat down at her desk.

"How are things?" he asked. "I wasn't sure if I should call you last night or not."

Jo felt a little guilty as she realised that by rights she should have called him. He had given up so much of his time yesterday to help her and she had not even thought to ring and thank him.

"It's just as well you didn't call really." She said, trying not to make too big an issue of it. "Things were a bit hectic." She told him what the doctor had said about Lee's condition and explained that Rick had taken her out to take her mind off it. She omitted to mention that her father had told her to let her brother die, and that Rick had apparently undergone a personality transplant. He listened to the news about Lee pensively, nodding as she spoke.

"It's standard practice now to ask those questions." He said. "They need to have permission to label someone DNAR. That way the hospital can avoid lawsuits if anything happens."

"DNAR? What's that?"

"Do Not Attempt Resuscitation. Suki's talked about it. She hates those situations. So what are you going to do?"

50

"I wish I knew, Jas. I really wish I knew." She stared at her computer screen as if seeking an answer there. Jas stood beside her and gently squeezed her shoulder.

"You'll do the right thing, I know you will." Josie placed her hand on top of his, grateful for his support.

At that moment, the door burst open and Pam breezed in, throwing her coat over the back of her chair. Jas moved his hand from Jo's shoulder and stepped back a little. Josie felt herself blushing slightly but Pam was oblivious to the situation as she poured her coffee and settled down to work. As Jas headed for his own office, Josie called the hospital to ask about Lee. There had been no change overnight so she arranged to meet with the consultant at five-thirty. As she ended the call, she prayed silently that she would know what to say by then.

*

"We have a duty to preserve life while we can Josie." The old priest was saying as he walked with her to the door. "But that doesn't necessarily mean it should be prolonged. If it's God's Will, Lee will recover, and if it's not well..." He seemed reluctant to complete the sentence.

Father Paul had been her parish priest for most of her life. He had officiated at her marriage, and he had baptised Susie. She had gone to the church at lunchtime to light a candle and pray for guidance. Father Paul had been there and she had sought his advice, but now as she thanked him for listening and headed back to work she realised he had not been as helpful as she had hoped.

"A duty to preserve life, not necessarily to prolong it?" Did that mean the doctors should keep Lee alive or not? She supposed that preserving life meant not switching off the machine that was breathing for Lee at the moment. So perhaps prolonging it meant resuscitating him if his heart stopped. They didn't necessarily have to do that.

She was no wiser than before. It seemed that even the Church could not tell her what was right. She had to face this choice alone.

Rick was as good as his word for a change and he arrived home at half-past four, just as Josie was making a pot of tea. She was glad that he was there and that she would not have to face the hospital alone. He went upstairs and returned a few minutes later having changed out of his suit into jeans and a sweatshirt. Josie gave him an appreciative look, admiring the fact that even in casual clothes he could always appear groomed and stylish. He was tall and broad-shouldered with a good physique apart from the beginnings of a middle-aged spread around the waist. He was the sort of man that people turned their heads to look at. Josie, on the other hand always seemed to struggle with her clothes. She felt that she could look OK on occasions, but never chic, smart, or beautiful. She felt too short, and her hair would never stay in place, so she often just tied it back out of the way.

They took Rick's car and arrived in plenty of time to spend half an hour at Lee's bedside before their appointment with the consultant. Rick stood looking out of the window while Josie stroked her brother's hair and held his hand. His skin felt cool and clammy. Tubes and wires connected him to various machines, which were keeping him breathing, and tracking his heart rate. Josie watched his face, desperately seeking any sign that he was about to wake up. Every so often, she noticed the movement beneath his eyelids that she believed was what they called REM sleep. She thought that she had read somewhere that this meant he was dreaming and she latched onto this idea as an indicator that maybe his brain was functioning well enough. Perhaps he was just asleep. "Come on Lee," she said softly. "You can get through this."

"It's no good. He can't hear you." Rick said, turning towards her. "You need to be strong and accept that."

"There's no harm in hoping." She whispered almost to herself. Rick looked at his watch.

"Well, it's time to see what the experts say." He took her arm as she got up and led her from the room.

The consultant reminded her of her father in some ways. He must have been approaching retirement and he looked as if it could not come soon enough. His office was spacious and embellished with the personal touches that showed its occupant had been in residence for a long time. Family photographs lined the window ledge behind his desk and two plants, which Josie could not identify, sat on a low table flanked by four soft-seated chairs. It was here that they were invited to sit.

"I am Mr Harrison and I have been overseeing your brother's care Mrs Anson. First of all, I have to tell you that the prognosis is not good at present, but I believe my colleague filled you in on that last night." His manner was somewhat abrupt, and Josie was taken aback.

"There's been no change then?" she asked.

"None. I realise this is very hard for you, but I prefer to be honest. At this point, it looks extremely unlikely that your brother will regain consciousness. The tests show very little sign of brain activity and he is unable to breathe independently." He looked at Josie to make sure she was taking this in before continuing. "There are two options available to you concerning how we proceed." He paused again. Josie found herself squeezing Rick's hand as the doctor went on to explain what he called her "options".

They could wait and see if Lee would wake up, keeping him alive with intravenous feeding and keeping him attached to all those machines or they could detach him from the machinery and let nature take its course. If she chose the second option, it would be on the understanding that there would be no attempt to resuscitate him when his breathing stopped or his heart failed as was sure to happen in due course.

53

Josie wept silently as she thought about it. Rick held her hands in his and said she must be sensible. She still had so many questions but she didn't know where to start and then Mr Harrison's pager bleeped and he apologised and ushered them into the waiting room, as he had to go and deal with an emergency. They sat drinking weak tea from the vending machine and after an hour a nurse told them that Mr Harrison sent his apologies; he would not be able to continue their discussions tonight. He asked if Josie could telephone him the next day and the nurse wrote down the number for the direct line to his secretary.

Outside the hospital Rick made his way directly to the shelter provided for smokers and lit a cigar. Josie watched as he inhaled and then reaching into her bag she pulled out the cigarettes she had brought with her from Lee's flat the day before. Rick stared in amazement and barely concealed disapproval as she lit one.

"When did you start that again?" he asked.

"Yesterday," she replied, "I found them at Lee's and I had one then." She felt self-conscious now.

"You know I don't like to see you smoking, Josie. It's unfeminine." Rick stubbed out his cigar and started walking towards the car park. Josie drew on the cigarette one more time before throwing it into the bucket of sand that served as an ashtray and following him.

As she got into the car, she could see that Rick was trying hard to control his temper. She placed a hand on his arm.

"I'm sorry, Rick, I just felt I needed something to calm me down and help me think straight."

He turned towards her, his face set and his expression hard. "I don't see what there is to think about really. The choice is obvious isn't it?"

"No it isn't - not to me."

The drive home took place in silence.

Chapter Eight

He was waking up; she was sure of it. Just a little flutter at the corner of the eyelid at first and then the flutter became a twitch. Finally, with a massive effort, both eyes forced themselves open and then closed again as the light flooded in. A few seconds, and they were open again - misty and vague to begin with, then clearing and looking around in confusion. At last, they focussed on Josie and the trace of a smile played around his mouth as if it couldn't quite remember how to form completely. Then the words came rushing out.

"Why are you crying, Sis? Did somebody die?"

Her head was aching and the pillow was damp beneath her face when she woke up. Rick came in from the bathroom with a towel wrapped around his waist, and began dressing for work. He tossed the damp towel playfully at her.

"Come on, Sleeping Beauty. You can't stay there all day."

Josie breathed a sigh of relief. He had obviously shaken off his anger from the night before.

"I'm on my way". She hauled herself out of bed and down to the kitchen where Rick had made coffee. She was thankful that there was no sign of a cooked breakfast this morning.

"Sorry I was such a grouch last night." Rick kissed her cheek as she sat down. "I just hate hospitals, and then seeing you smoking again, well it was the final straw."

"I know, love. I'm sorry too. I won't do it again."

"Good girl. Why don't I take the cigarettes with me, then you won't be tempted?"

Josie sighed. "They're in my bag."

Rick went through to the living room and returned with the handbag. He opened it and took out the cigarettes. Pausing briefly, he put his hand back into the bag and brought out a piece of paper. Josie swallowed hard as she recognised the note Jas had left for her at the hospital on Wednesday. Rick read it and placed it in front of her on the table.

"What's this?" His voice was icy. "Why is your boss sending you secret notes?"

"It's not like that. He'd been helping me find Lee. He left when Dad arrived. He was concerned." She could see that he didn't believe her. Why hadn't she thrown the note away? Rick was staring at her with something akin to disgust.

"You expect me to believe that, I suppose. Well, little Miss Innocent, that seems like more than friendly concern to me. That man wants more than friendship from you and I'm sure you're encouraging him all the way!" Without giving her a chance to reply he stormed out of the house slamming the door behind him.

Josie stared after him. This was too much. He couldn't seriously think that she and Jas were ... She couldn't complete the sentence, even in her own mind; it was so unfair. Jas had shown her nothing but kindness. He had been there for her when Rick had been off with the latest one, whoever she was. Rick could think what he chose to about Josie, but accusing Jas was just wrong. She was sure his friendship had no ulterior motive. He was simply a good man and that was something Rick would never be able to understand.

Her anger surprised her. When these scenes had occurred before she had felt differently. There had been tears and self-doubt. She didn't know where this fury had come from but it was somehow comforting. She felt strong for a change as she decided she would not call Rick later to try and sort things out. Let him be the first to admit defeat.

As she dressed for work, her dream came back to her. It had seemed so real that she wondered if perhaps it was some kind of omen. She would call the hospital later and arrange another meeting with the consultant. Maybe they would tell her that Lee had regained consciousness. Even though she knew this was unlikely, the thought cheered her up.

She opened the door to Susie's room to say goodbye. Susie was sleeping fitfully and still looked pale. Josie decided not to disturb her, but resolved that tonight she would set aside some "girl time". The trauma of the last few days had left little space for that and it had always been an important part of her relationship with her daughter. She closed the door quietly and left the house, heading once again for the only place where things went according to plan.

Josie had just sat down at her desk when Pam rang to say that she wouldn't be coming in to work. She sounded weak as she explained that a "dodgy" curry had left her with a stomach upset. Josie sympathised and told her to take care. Ten minutes later Jas popped his head around the door to say that he had arrived. Josie passed on the news about Pam and he nodded.

"Poor Pam. Still, it'll probably pass off in a couple of hours. How are things with you?"

"Could be better, I suppose. No change with Lee." She was trying not to sound too depressed but it was difficult. Sensing that she did not feel like making conversation Jas withdrew to his office and Josie started looking through the pile of commissions in her inbox. She was soon caught up in her work and the verses flowed across her screen to be captured and saved in the appropriate folders: birth, marriage, death, illness, success, goodbye, good luck, I'm sorry. There were so many occasions people wanted cards for that she could be doing this forever. Was that what she really wanted from life? At this moment, she thought it probably was.

At eleven o'clock, she telephoned the hospital and was told that there was still no change in Lee's condition. Mr. Harrison was not available to see her until Monday so she accepted the offered appointment, and said she would be in to see Lee over the weekend.

Jas came and helped himself to a cup of coffee, then sat down at Pam's desk, glancing through the sketches she had been working on.

"They're so good." He said. "Like your verses. What a team we are!" Josie found herself smiling and agreeing.

"The best."

"Absolutely. Our finest quality of course is our humility."

Josie was laughing now, "Welcome to the "Jasuprint Mutual Admiration Society.""

Jas raised his coffee mug in a mock toast. "May we never be guilty of false modesty!"

"I'd drink to that," said Jo, "but my cup's empty."

"Then share mine." Jas stood up to pass her the coffee. She took the cup and sipped from it before handing it back, feeling almost embarrassed for no reason that she could explain. Jas finished the contents in one gulp and then with a dramatic bow he swept out of the room. Josie stared after him for a while. She wasn't sure exactly what had just happened. It seemed somehow more significant than a little banter. It had been almost like flirting. She decided to put it out of her mind and get on with her work.

An hour later Jas was back in the room. He took Josie's jacket from the coat stand in the corner and handed it to her.

"It's time for the meeting." He said.

"What meeting? I don't remember any meeting."

Jas looked sheepish. "That's because I've only just arranged it." he said. "The manager at 'The Crown' has some work for us, so I said we'd go there for lunch." He saw

58

her hesitation. "Unless of course you have other plans. It is short notice."

"No, I don't have plans, but what about the office? Supposing there are calls?" She was aware that she was procrastinating but she didn't know why. Jas reached across her desk and turned on the answering machine. Josie found herself blushing as she logged off her computer and pulled on her jacket. She realised that Rick's accusations had made her start to doubt the nature of Jas's friendship and the anger she had felt this morning returned. She resolved that she was not going to let it get the better of her.

"OK, Boss. I'm ready." She said.

"That's great, because I'm starving." Jas was already halfway out of the door.

The Crown was just across the road from the office. It was a popular venue for business lunches as they served good food, Real Ale and quality wines. They found a table and Jas fetched their drinks from the bar and brought two menus.

"Ted will be joining us in a few minutes. He's supervising a delivery apparently. We're to order whatever we fancy – it's on the house."

"That's nice. Is he after a big favour?"

"Just some invitations for his daughter's wedding, I believe, but I think he needs them in a hurry."

They studied the menus in silence and after a few minutes, the landlord came over and took their order personally. He relayed the details to the bar staff and then joined them at the table. They discussed the order for the invitations. Ted explained that he needed them in two weeks and that he wanted them to be very special. His daughter was the star in his heaven and everything had to be perfect.

"We won't let you down." said Jas. "My creative team is the best in the business." Ted grinned at him.

"And very modest too, I'm sure." He said. At this, Jas and Josie both laughed remembering their earlier conversation. Jas promised to have a draft ready for Ted's approval by Monday and they shook hands as the landlord went back to his duties and their lunch arrived. The food lived up to its reputation and Josie finally began to relax. Jas was good company and they moved easily through various topics of conversation. Jas asked about her family and as she told him all about Susie he sighed.

"It sounds like you have a great relationship with your daughter, Jo. You're very lucky."

"I suppose I am. She's wonderful." and before she knew it she was asking him about his family. She knew nothing at all of his personal life and it had never seemed right to ask before.

"I have a son, Rajinder. He's the same age as your Susie, but our relationship's not as good as yours."

"Some lads get on better with their mothers at that age."

"Maybe, but my boy's mother left us when he was five. He's always blamed me for it although he knows nothing about it."

For the first time Josie detected a trace of bitterness in Jas. Perhaps this was why he had never spoken about his family life before.

"Can't you explain to him? Give him the facts."

Jas looked uncomfortable.

"Maybe I should have done that long ago. It might be too late now." Before Josie could reply, Jas changed the subject. "Well, I really enjoyed lunch, but I have some calls to make so we should get back to the office."

He left a generous tip on the table and helped Josie into her jacket. As they made their way towards the exit, the sound of laughter made her look to her left. Jas saw the expression on her face as she suddenly pushed past him and went out into the street. He hurried and caught up with her as she was crossing the road. She was breathing hard and her

60

face was flushed. He walked with her, but didn't say anything until they were back at work.

"Was it something I said?" He asked as she took her seat in front of the computer. Josie looked at him in surprise.

"No, of course not. I just saw someone that I knew in the pub. That's all."

"And you got upset."

"Yes, but I'm OK now, really."

Jas patted her shoulder as he headed for his own office.

"You know where I am if you need me, Jo."

She checked the answering machine –there was only a message from Pam saying she'd be back tomorrow, and then she logged on to continue working, but her heart was not in it. She could not shake the image from her mind. The laughing couple in the pub had been all over each other, his arm around her, her hand resting on his knee as they shared their joke. She had been gazing up into his eyes, eyes that Josie knew so well, Rick's eyes. Josie tried to find consolation in the fact that he hadn't seen her having lunch with Jas, but it didn't help and now the hurt she had suffered on and off for so many years felt different because it was mixed with anger and maybe even the beginnings of rebellion.

Chapter Nine

Your pain is my pain; your tears are my own.
From baby to woman – how fast time has flown.

(From Josie's Journal – Cards for all Occasions)

Jo and Susie settled down with the TV guide and a pizza. Rick had called to say that he would not require dinner, so the planned girls' night was able to go ahead. Susie was quiet at first, feigning interest in the television. Josie recognised the tactics and eventually took the remote control and switched off the set

"Talk to me Susie," she said, "I know something's on your mind, and I know that I've been preoccupied with Lee lately, but I love you and I know when things aren't right." She could see that her daughter was holding back tears. "Let it go, love, talk to me."

The girl's tears came in torrents. There were no words at first, just huge gulps and sobs as she clung to her mother. Then at last, she managed to speak.

"It's Pete. He's with her all the time now, and I miss him so much. I loved him Mum, I really loved him."

"I know you did, sweetheart. Love can be a real pain."

"I thought he loved me. I was sure he loved me. Oh what am I going to do?" Her distress was tearing at her mother's heart. She thought of Peter and saw Rick's face. She struggled to find the right thing to say. She felt she wasn't qualified to talk about love and relationships when her own was in such a poor state.

"You have to try and be strong, darling. I know it's hard to believe, but you will get over it eventually. You'll find someone who'll deserve you."

At this, Susie cried harder. "Who's going to want me?" she sobbed. "I've messed up everything. I'm so sorry."

"There's nothing for you to be sorry for, Susie. You've done nothing wrong, love."

Susie's eyes met her mother's at last.

"But I have." She said. "I think I might be pregnant."

Jo was stunned into silence for moment. She had never considered the possibility that Susie and Peter had slept together. Her daughter seemed such an innocent, and still so young in many ways. Of course she knew that attitudes to sex were different now, and that teenagers started to be active much younger, but she hadn't expected this from Susie. She looked at her little girl who was now covering her face with her hands, and as the shock passed off it was replaced with overwhelming love and a desire to protect her child from any further pain. She drew the girl into her arms and held her close.

"It will be OK; everything will be fine. I'll take care of you. Don't worry." As she said the words, she thought again of Rick and knew that there would be tough times ahead. Well, that would have to wait. Right now, she had other priorities – her daughter and possibly her grandchild would have to come first.

Later, when Susie had gone to bed and Rick still had not returned. Josie had time to think seriously about Susie's revelation. She realised with some surprise that she was not angry or upset by the news, and now that she was over the initial shock, she quite enjoyed the thought of being a grandmother. That is if Susie was actually pregnant. It was all rather circumstantial at the moment. She had been feeling sick; her period was a week late and she had not used any form of contraception when she had slept with Peter for the first time two months ago. It had also been the last time, according to Susie. She had been plagued by guilt and had not been in a hurry to repeat the experience. This reluctance had probably contributed to Peter's seeking satisfaction elsewhere. Josie decided they would buy a home testing kit the next day. There could be no planning until they knew for sure.

She glanced at her watch. It was only ten o'clock and it felt too early to go to bed on a Friday night. She flicked through the channels on the TV and rejected them all. Finally deciding that music would be good for her she put on a CD of soft jazz played on a saxophone. She sipped hot chocolate and closed her eyes.

The nurse was singing as she wheeled Jo down to the operating theatre. Jo could barely make out the words through the fog in her brain. The little blue pill they had given her was doing its job. She was hardly aware of the pain now, but she could remember it. She knew she would never forget it. Hot and searing through her abdomen, making her feel weak and helpless. She wanted to cry again, but there were no tears left in her and Rick had gone. She felt empty and soon she would be. They were taking away the child that was not meant to be. They could call it what they liked, she thought. Dress it up in any old medical term, but it was still her child and she would grieve for it.

Susie was three years old and they had discussed having another baby. It was too early to confirm it, but Jo was sure she was pregnant. She hadn't told Rick yet, it was too early. Then the pain came, that dreadful pain that told her something was very wrong. She fought against it; convinced herself that she had food poisoning or something. It would go away and all would be well, but after a few hours, she had to call Rick. A scan revealed an ectopic pregnancy. There would be no happy ending here. Rick could not cope with her distress and left her there, saying he had to get Susie from his sister's. He did not visit until three days later. The doctors said that Josie could still have more children if she chose to, although she had lost a fallopian tube, but neither she nor Rick ever brought up the subject again, tacitly agreeing that Susie would be an only child.

As the CD finished, Jo opened her eyes. Her cheeks were moist and she thought it strange it that even after all these years the memory saddened her. She went upstairs and looked in at her sleeping child, saying a silent prayer that all would be well.

Saturday morning came and Josie was glad for once that Rick had spent the night in the spare room. She did not want to see him or talk to him at present. There was far too much going on in her mind. Susie's bedroom door was open and the sound of running water from the bathroom told Josie that her daughter was taking a shower. This was good; it meant that they could go out early and avoid Rick for a while longer.

Josie made coffee and warmed some croissants, and when Susie came downstairs in her blue terry bathrobe, the kitchen smelt like a Parisian café. She looked more relaxed than she had for days. Her eyes were clear and sparkling and she had styled her hair, still damp from the shower into a French plait.

"This is great, Mum," she said, sitting down and taking a massive bite from a croissant, followed by a mouthful of coffee.

"You look a lot better today. No morning sickness?" asked Josie. Susie swallowed hard and grinned at her mother.

"False alarm. My 'little friend' arrived this morning." This was the way they had referred to periods when Susie had been younger. "Sorry to have worried you. If I'd kept my mouth shut for another day you could have been spared that trauma. I never thought I'd be so delighted to feel these lousy cramps!"

Josie took her hand and held it. She was lost for words, unsure of her own feelings. Of course, it was the best outcome really, but she could not help feeling just a little disappointed.

"That's good, love." She managed. "I'm glad you're OK."

They finished their breakfast and decided to go into town to celebrate with some retail therapy.

Rick came down just as they were preparing to leave the house. He grunted at them not to spend too much money, then switched on the TV and was instantly engrossed in the News with nothing further to say.

Two hours later, as Josie sat at a table in Starbuck's, surrounded by carrier bags, she heard a familiar voice.

"I must be paying you too much!" She looked up and smiled. Jas was casually dressed in jeans and a pale blue polo shirt with a leather jacket. Josie had never seen him in anything other than the suits he wore to work. The casual look suited him well; it made him look younger somehow. His thick dark hair showed no trace of grey, and in keeping with the weekend 'look', it was free from the styling gel that usually kept it slicked back. As a consequence, it had fallen naturally into a side parting with a half-fringe. The only lines on his face were around his eyes and mouth. Jo's mother would have called them "laughter lines". She found herself wondering how old he actually was. It was yet another thing she didn't know about him and of course it was not the sort of question she could ask.

"May I?" he asked, indicating one of the spare chairs. Josie nodded and he sat down just as Susie returned with two iced coffees, looking curiously at her mother's companion.

"This is my daughter, Susie. Susie this is Jas, my boss." Jas shook hands with Susie.

"How like your mother you are. How are the studies going?"

Susie was pleased that he showed an interest, and soon found herself telling him that she hoped to study creative writing at University next year. He smiled at her and turned to Josie.

"So you've passed your talent on as well as your beauty, Jo. You must be very proud of her."

Josie blushed furiously. She hoped Susie wouldn't make too much of Jas's elaborate compliments; she supposed it was a cultural thing. They spent a very pleasant half-hour together over coffee before parting company.

"Wow!" said Susie as soon as Jas was out of earshot and they were walking back to the car park. "He's really nice Mum, and so fit! No wonder you love your job." Josie found herself blushing as she admonished her daughter.

"He's a kind man and a good boss. I've never thought of him any other way." She tried to sound indignant. Susie laughed.

"I'm only teasing, but, jokes apart, if he was a bit younger I'd have a hard job not thinking about him. He's real eye candy."

They had reached the car and Josie did not reply.

Chapter Ten

I can't write, I can't think.
(From Josie's Journal –Cards for all Occasions)

Josie received the message as she left St. Jude's after Mass on Sunday morning. Her phone was switched off during the service and she had just taken it out to turn it on. The text message informed her that she had a new voice mail and she quickly selected the option to retrieve it. Susie watched her face as she listened to the message and ended the call. The colour drained away and she looked distressed.

"What's up Mum?"

"I'm not sure. I have to phone the hospital as soon as possible. It's something to do with Lee." She started to dial the number but Susie stopped her.

"Ten minutes won't hurt. Let's go home first. Call from there." She was right of course. They always walked to Church as it was only a short distance from the house. If Josie had to go to the hospital, she would need to take the car. They walked briskly and in silence. Rick's car had gone. He had obviously got up and gone out while they were at Mass.

Susie went into the kitchen to make coffee while Josie made the phone call. She spoke to the ward sister. She was silent for a long time as she listened and finally she said quietly "I'll be there shortly; within the hour." Putting the phone down, she looked up as Susie came in with her coffee. She tried to speak, but words wouldn't come out and all she could manage was a strangled sob which hurt her chest and throat. The tears that were sure to follow were slow in coming and for several minutes she was wracked by dry, harsh sobs and tremors. She had never known such heartache; it was worse than physical pain. Susie held her, instinctively rocking her back and forth like a child. There had still been no words, but none were necessary. Susie could guess what the news had been.

When the sobs eased and the tears came, Susie took control, urging her mother to drink her coffee and picking up the phone to call Rick's mobile. It was switched off, of course, so she left a curt message.

"Dad, call me as soon as you get this. It's urgent."

Josie was beginning to calm down and was drying her eyes and blowing her nose.

"What happens now, Mum?" Susie asked.

"I need to go to the hospital to see him one last time before they move him." Her voice was still thick with tears. She got to her feet and picked up the car keys.

"You can't drive, Mum. You're too upset. Let me call a taxi." It was not really a request but an order and Josie was grateful that Susie was being so practical. She sat down and awaited further instruction, unwilling and unable to think for herself.

Standing at the bedside, with the curtains drawn around them, Josie forced herself to open her eyes and look at Lee. It seemed like a cliché to think that he looked peaceful, but that was her first thought. The tubes and wires that had supported his life for the last few days had been removed. They had been rendered unnecessary when his heart had stopped beating despite their electronic intervention. He lay as if asleep and his sister gazed with love and sadness on the face that in death seemed to have regained some of its youthful beauty. The redness of his cheeks and nose had faded when the blood ceased flowing. He appeared relaxed and at ease.

She bent down and placed her lips against his cold forehead, whispering as she had when they were children, "Goodnight, sleep tight, don't let the bedbugs bite." She realised how foolish it sounded, but she knew that somewhere, somehow Lee would understand. As she

69

straightened up a large tear landed on Lee's eyelid. She turned away at last, unable to bear the thought that she would never again be cheered by the sight of those blue eyes sparkling with mischief, or share in one of his quirky jokes.

She made the sign of the Cross and tried to pray as she knew she should "Eternal rest give unto him, oh Lord .." she could not continue as the tears overwhelmed her and then she felt her daughter's arms around her and heard Susie take over.

"And let Perpetual Light shine upon him. May he rest in peace."

Josie managed to join her to say "Amen."

Drawing the curtain back slightly, Susie led her mother away from the bedside to the nurses' station where the ward sister again expressed her sympathy and handed them a folder containing what she called 'information they might find helpful'. Outside the hospital, Susie checked her phone and Josie's. There had been no message from Rick so she tried calling him again. This time it rang twice and he answered impatiently.

"Susie, I'm in the middle of something here. I can't talk to you now."

"You have to, Dad. Mum's in a bad way – Uncle Lee died. We're just leaving the hospital. Please meet us at home."

Rick sounded exasperated. He said that he would do his best, but he didn't know how long he would be. He told her to go home and look after her mother like a good girl and then he ended the call without giving her a chance to say anything else. Susie stared at the phone in disbelief for a moment and then called a taxi.

Back at home, Josie lay down on the sofa and was soon sleeping fitfully. Every so often, she would sob or moan as she turned from side to side. Susie watched her for a while and then decided to make herself useful. She looked through the information provided by the hospital and made a list of the things that would have to be done on Monday. They would have to register the death and obtain a death certificate and then start to make funeral arrangements. It was now two hours since she'd phoned Rick and he still hadn't appeared. She thought about calling him again, but once she had the phone in her hand, she changed her mind. He would be here in his own time and rushing him wouldn't help; it would just mean that he would be in a foul mood when he arrived.

Josie stirred and opened her eyes. She smiled weakly at Susie and asked if Rick was home yet. Susie shook her head and asked hesitantly if she could phone her grandfather. Josie's eyes filled with tears again.

"I should have thought of that sooner." She said. "Yes call him straight away. Tell him I'm sorry and I need to see him." She wasn't ready to talk to Joe in person so she went into the kitchen while Susie made the call.

Looking out of the window at the garden, she spotted a cat stalking a sparrow. It looked like a stray; a scrawny creature with scruffy black fur and white paws. Cats usually take better care of themselves, she thought. This one was a sorry sight indeed. On impulse, she took some cold chicken from the fridge and put it into a dish. Opening the door quietly so she wouldn't scare him off, she placed the dish on the patio and waited. The cat eyed her curiously and then wandered over nonchalantly and sniffed at the meat. When he realised it was meant for him he started wolfing it down greedily. Josie knelt down and stroked him as he ate. He had no collar and certainly hadn't been eating well. Josie fetched him a saucer of milk and that disappeared rapidly too. By this time, the cat was purring with delight and winding himself around Josie's legs. She picked him up and carried him back into the kitchen where she sat cuddling him and gazing into space.

"Granddad will be here tomorrow evening." Susie came into the kitchen and sat facing her mother. "Who's this?"

Josie snapped out of her reverie and looked at the cat sleeping in her arms, like a baby.

"He's a stray and I'm keeping him and his name's Horatio." She sounded childlike and almost defiant. Susie wondered if Josie had been expecting an argument.

"That's great; I've always wanted a pet."

"So have I." Josie carried the cat into the living room and placed him in Rick's favourite chair.

Rick and Horatio did not hit it off very well to say the least. When the master of the house finally arrived to console his grieving wife, he was not at all impressed to find a cat in his chair. His attempt to evict the usurper was greeted with a snarl and a scratch across the back of his hand. Fuming, he turned to Josie but something in her expression stopped him from saying anything. He offered his condolences about Lee as if she were a stranger and asked what would happen next.

"I have to register the death and arrange the funeral, I suppose, but I can't do any of that until tomorrow." Her voice was flat now as if there was no emotion left in her. She felt numb inside. Rick sat beside her on the sofa and she moved towards him. He put his arm around her, but she felt as if the gesture was mechanical. She rested her head on his shoulder, but stiffened as she became aware of the fragrance that lingered there and was not hers.

"Where were you today, Rick?" She didn't really want to know the answer, but the question had to be asked. Rick's moment of hesitation was answer enough.

"Playing golf." He replied, but Josie wasn't listening. She was deep in thought. Eventually there would be a confrontation, but this wasn't the time; she wasn't strong enough yet.

Susie called from the kitchen to say that dinner was ready and they sat down to a meal of cold chicken, salad and

French bread. It was rare these days for the three of them to dine together and for Susie's sake Josie forced herself to eat although she had no appetite. Horatio curled up by her feet and was rewarded with frequent treats.

After dinner, somewhat predictably, Rick received a call and had to go out. Susie took the address book from the shelf by the phone and started to make a list of the people who should be informed of Lee's death. It was quite a short list. There were a few cousins in Liverpool and an elderly uncle in Wolverhampton. There had been little contact with any of them, other than Christmas cards, for a long time, so she supposed that there would not be many attending the funeral. The list complete, she looked at Josie who was once again nursing Horatio.

"Mum, are you going to phone Jas and tell him you won't be in for a while?"

Josie stared at her blankly for a moment as if she couldn't quite understand what she was being asked.

"I suppose so." She reached out and picked up her mobile. "No, I'll text. I can't talk to anyone now." She tapped the message into her phone and checked it before pressing "SEND". It looked cold and harsh in print on the little screen.

Won't be in 2moro. Lee died this am.

She could do nothing to make it sound any better, so she sent the message. As an afterthought, she copied it to Pam. Then, without another word she went upstairs and ran a deep and foamy bath, in the hope that she could somehow soak away the pain and misery that she was feeling; after all it worked for backache – was the heart really so different?

Chapter Eleven

*The remarkable blue eyes were looking straight at her
and she was meeting their gaze with wonder. Annie was just
as she remembered her; she hadn't aged at all. A glossy
mass of dark brown curls framed an almost elfin face. Her
lips, a perfect cupid's bow, were smiling, and above her
sharp little nose, the warmest, gentlest eyes revealed a
mixture of love and sadness. No words were spoken, but
Josie could hear her mother's voice inside her head.*

*"Don't cry, little Jo. I hate to see you cry." and then
"He's here with me. I was so lonely." Jo wanted to reply but
Annie's voice came again "Take care little Jo, be happy."
and then she was gone.*

Josie opened her eyes, surprised to realise that it was
morning already. She had slept for ten hours and she could
hear movement downstairs. She had no idea what time he
had come home last night, once she had fallen asleep at nine
o'clock she had not stirred. Hearing the sound of raised
voices she got up and went down to the kitchen. She listened
at the door for a moment. Susie was obviously very angry.
She hardly ever argued with her father.

"I don't care, Dad. You left us alone yesterday when
Mum really needed your support. You should have been
here."

"I came home when you asked me to." Rick sounded
sulky.

"You came home several hours later and as soon as
you could, you went out again. What is it with you these
days? Don't you want to be around us any more?" Susie's
voice was cracking. Josie had heard enough; she opened the
door and the argument stopped.

"What's up?" she asked.

"It's nothing for you to worry about, is it Dad?" Susie
turned away to make coffee. Rick agreed with her.

74

"That's good, because I've got enough to do without you two arguing today. What time will you be home Rick? I'll be cooking dinner for seven o'clock; Dad should be here by then."

Rick hesitated briefly, looking uncomfortable.

"I should be back by then." He said finally, then picking up his jacket he left for work.

"How are you feeling, Mum?" Susie asked.

"I'm OK, love. What time do you have to be in college? I can give you a lift if you like. I have to go into town to the register office and the undertaker anyway."

"I thought I'd take the day off and help you organise everything. You can't be expected to do it all yourself." Josie was shaking her head.

"I can't let you do that, Susie. You've got your exams in a few weeks, besides I need to be busy. I can manage this. If you want to help you can make some phone calls for me tonight." She sounded very sure of herself and Susie realised there would be no point arguing about it. Josie was looking around her. "Where's Horatio?"

Susie didn't know. She had forgotten all about him. They tried calling him, but there was no sign of him in the house or garden. After a few minutes, Josie decided to give up the search, but she left a saucer of milk outside anyway. She was sure he wouldn't have deserted her.

Having dropped Susie at college, Josie continued on to the Register Office. There was quite a queue at the reception desk, but fortunately a new system had just been introduced which gave priority to those who were registering deaths. It only took 20 minutes for Josie to see the registrar and obtain the death certificate. By eleven o'clock, she had made the necessary arrangements with the funeral directors and Father Paul. Lee would be received into St. Jude's on the following Monday evening and the requiem Mass would take place on Tuesday afternoon.

The message light on the answering machine was flashing when Josie arrived home. There had been four messages, according to the digital display. Josie decided she would need a drink before listening to them. She poured a measure of vodka into a large glass and added a generous helping of lemonade before pressing "play". The first message was from a firm who wanted to offer a free quotation for cavity wall insulation; she deleted it. Then she heard Rick's voice.

"I tried your mobile, but the bloody thing's off. I can't get home this evening. There's a meeting in Manchester I have to go to. I'll call in the morning."

Josie's anger surprised her. "Bastard!" she yelled at the phone. She was about to switch the machine off when the next message started. It was Jas, his voice soft and full of sympathy.

"Jo, I'm so sorry about your brother. If there's anything I can do, call me. Take as much time as you need."

The strength that had stayed with her all morning was beginning to evaporate now and she felt lonely and sad. The final message was from Pam, timed just before Josie arrived home.

"Jo, I'm on my way round. Jas has given me the afternoon off. Did you know your mobile's off? If you're not back when I get there I'm going to wait so you'll see me before you get this message. God! I hate these machines; they make you say stupid things!"

Jo took her mobile out of her bag and switched it on. There was a list of missed calls from Rick, Pam, Jas and her father. Joe had left no message, so steeling herself for a difficult time she called his mobile.

"Little Jo" he said as soon as he answered the phone. "I'm so sorry love. I should never have left you to deal with this."

"It's OK Dad. It's all forgotten. Where are you?"

"I'm having lunch at a service station near Oxford. I came over in the car in case there was any running about to do. I should be there in a couple of hours." Josie was tearful now; she couldn't wait to see him.

"Thanks, Dad. I love you."

"I love you too, little Jo. Hang on in there. I won't be long."

The call ended and Jo took a huge gulp from her drink. It really wasn't helping. The doorbell rang and Pam stood there with her arms full of tulips and daffodils and her eyes full of tears. Josie ushered her into the kitchen and Pam put down her burdens and hugged her fiercely.

"Oh Jo, what can I say? I know how much he meant to you. Can I do anything for you? Are you OK?" With each question Pam's embrace seemed to grow tighter. Josie pulled away slightly, afraid she wouldn't be able to breathe if Pam showed any more concern.

"Thanks. I'll be OK, but it'll take a while. The flowers are lovely. It's very thoughtful of you."

"They're not from me," Pam was taking off her jacket and throwing it over the back of a chair. "Jas sent them; that's why it's such an odd assortment. Men are hopeless when it comes to choosing flowers." She opened her handbag. "I brought you something more useful." She produced an enormous bar of chocolate. "Medical evidence suggests that chocolate is a great anti-depressant."

Josie managed a smile, only Pam would think of chocolate as an antidote to the poison of bereavement. She made tea and they sat in the garden, making the most of the warm afternoon. Pam was cautious at first, as she assessed how Josie was coping, but caution didn't sit well on her and soon she was in full flow.

"I've finished with Mark." She announced. "He was beginning to get on my nerves with all that attention and stuff. I didn't escape from Ratbag to get involved with another needy bloke."

Josie was fascinated in spite of herself. "I thought you were having a great time." She said.

"Well, it was good for a few weeks, but he started to get too serious. I mean, on Friday night he said he loved me. It worried me that much I couldn't sleep."

"Why?"

"Jo, I was in love once, with my ex, and it's not that great. When you love someone completely like that, it leaves you open to being hurt. I'm not going down that road again. I suppose I could have loved Mark, given time, but right now I just want to have some fun."

Josie nodded; she thought she understood. There was a rustling sound from the bush at the bottom of the garden and suddenly Horatio appeared at top speed and leapt onto Josie's lap, knocking her teacup to the ground where it shattered. She hugged the cat and laughed.

"This is the new man in my life." She explained. Pam laughed and stroked the cat, who stretched and purred, loving the fuss. "Horatio, say hello to Auntie Pam."

"Doesn't he mind about the others?" Pam asked mischievously.

"Well, he doesn't really get on with Rick."

"What about Jas?" She was looking pointedly at Josie who found herself blushing for no good reason.

"What about him? He's never met my cat." She put the cat down and started to pick up the broken crockery.

"You can tell me, Jo. What's going on with you and Jas? I'd have to be blind not to notice the signs." Pam seemed quite serious for a change. "You race off one day to sort Lee out and Jas follows. Next thing I know he calls to tell me neither of you will be back. I come into the office the next day and silence falls. I phone at lunchtime the day I'm off sick and the answerphone's on. Then I walk past Starbuck's on Saturday and there the two of you are tête à tête."

Josie stared at her. She could suddenly see that all these events were certainly open to misinterpretation. She didn't quite know what to say.

"Susie was there on Saturday, we bumped into Jas and he joined us. He's been a really good friend to me, Pam. Please don't try to suggest it's any more than that." She went inside to put the broken cup in the kitchen bin and realised her hands were shaking. By the time she sat down outside again she was fighting back tears. Pam was distraught.

"Oh Jo; I was only teasing. I didn't mean to upset you. Me and my big mouth! I'm supposed to be cheering you up." Jo was crying openly now.

"I know. I'm just feeling over-sensitive." She sobbed. Pam took her hand and squeezed it gently.

"Of course you are, love, and I guess I'm just a bit jealous that our hunky boss has been looking after you."

Josie managed a little laugh. "Hunky? Jas? I hadn't thought of him that way."

Now it was Pam's turn to laugh. "You mean you haven't noticed those chocolate bar eyes? What did that TV advert say? 'Full of eastern promise' – that's our Jas!"

Josie's tears had stopped now. "I should have known that chocolate would enter into it somewhere!" She said, and opening the chocolate that Pam had brought with her she successfully closed the subject.

Chapter Twelve

Am I losing my mind, or just losing control?
Am I falling to pieces or am I still whole?
Please don't think me a fool, though it's foolish I seem.
Did I say it aloud, or was it just a dream?

(From Josie's Journal – Cards for all Occasions)

The next week passed quickly; there was so much to organise. Looking back, Josie could never quite remember how they had done it all. Joe and Susie made phone calls, cooked meals and did the shopping. Rick came home from work every day, but spent most of the evenings working on the computer. He was sleeping in the spare room again, so Susie had moved in with Josie and given her room to her grandfather for the duration of his visit.

Josie spent a lot of time in a daze. She wandered about the house looking for something to occupy her thoughts, but her concentration failed often and she could not complete anything. Wherever she went, Horatio was not far behind her. Seeming to sense her unhappiness, he followed her, twisting himself around her ankles and as soon as she sat down he would settle on her lap demanding fuss. He was looking healthier now that he was eating regularly and he was grooming himself properly. Josie thought he was a very handsome cat and she was well on the way to spoiling him completely.

Pam came over several times and helped. Joe and Susie were very grateful when she offered to prepare a buffet for the small reception that was to take place after the funeral. There would only be about twenty people coming. Susie had traced a few of Lee's old school friends through the internet and two of them had emailed to say they would attend; the rest would be mainly family.

The night before the funeral, Jas phoned. It was the first time Josie had spoken to him since Lee's death. She had been diverting all her calls and sending texts in response to voice mails. Realising she had to start talking to people eventually, she answered the call. His voice was gentle and somehow comforting as he greeted her.

"Jo, I'm so glad you took the call. Pam's been keeping me informed but I wanted to hear for myself how you are."

"I'm getting there, but it's tough." She said. "I'll be back at work on Wednesday for what it's worth."

"It's worth a great deal, Jo. We've missed you." He paused for a moment before continuing, "I don't really know the conventions in your religion, but I was wondering if you'd mind if I came to your brother's funeral? Is that allowed? I'd like to pay my respects."

Josie was moved by this unexpected request and she was also aware of how much she had missed Jas for the last week.

"That's fine, Jas. You'll be very welcome, and thanks; I appreciate the thought. Shall I give you the details?"

"I took the liberty of getting all the info from Pam," He sounded slightly embarrassed. "She was sure you'd agree, but I felt I should ask anyway."

"Good old Pam. Well, I'll see you in church then."

The funeral service and cremation were over. It seemed strange that so few people could have shed so many tears. Josie and her father had held onto each other throughout, supported by Susie. Rick had been there in the background, playing the role expected of him without a great deal of conviction. Josie knew that he felt no grief about Lee and these days his attention was always somewhere else. She doubted if he had even noticed how deeply the loss had impacted on her or even on Susie who had been fond of her uncle.

Now they were back at home with a houseful of well-wishers, and Rick had been called away yet again. Pam had taken care of the catering and there was a splendid buffet laid out in kitchen. In the living room there were drinks of all kinds set out for people to help themselves to. Conversations were hushed as memories of Lee were exchanged, and occasionally there would be laughter, quickly stifled as the guests wondered if it was appropriate to laugh at such a time.

Big Joe and Susie acted as hosts; Josie accepted condolences with a nod and a weak smile. After a little while, she slipped away to the bathroom. Catching sight of her reflection in the full-length mirror, she almost failed to recognise herself. Recent events had taken their toll on her and it seemed as if every worry she had ever had was now etched on her face. Her red-rimmed eyes had a sunken appearance and their sparkle had dulled; the natural pink of her rounded cheeks had faded to a tired and insipid beige, leaving just two splotches of colour along the top of her cheekbones. Even her usually full lips seemed to have narrowed and her laughter lines had deepened into wrinkles.

She washed her face in cold water, patted it dry with a soft towel and then pinched her cheeks in an attempt to restore the colour, without much success. She did not want to look like an old woman, even if that was how she felt. On impulse, she went into the bedroom and applied some make up, and a little "L'Aimant" perfume. Finally, feeling a little more presentable, she rejoined the company downstairs.

Jas and Pam were in the kitchen clearing the table of empty plates and washing up used glasses. Horatio was winding himself around Jas's legs as he stood at the sink. As Jo came in, the cat ran to her.

"You shouldn't be doing that. We'll take care of it later"

"It's OK, Jo. We came to be useful." said Pam.

"Anyway, it's nearly finished." Jas rinsed out the last glass, placed it on the draining board and dried his hands. "Can I get you a cup of tea or anything?"

Josie realised that she hadn't eaten since early morning and it was now six o'clock; she was starving. She also needed a drink. Jas brought the bottle of vodka from the living room and poured drinks for the three of them adding ice and orange juice. Pam piled a plate with sausage rolls, cold meat and potato salad and handed it to Josie. Horatio looked on greedily and followed as they went out into the garden taking the bottle with them. It was late April and the weather was unusually warm for the time of year, making it a very good time to sit outside. Jo thanked them for all their help.

"I don't know how I'd have managed without Susie, Dad and you two. I've been useless for the last week." She put her plate down so that Horatio could finish her leftovers, and poured more vodka into her glass. She downed it quickly and finally started to feel its effect.

"Where did Rick disappear to?" Pam, never a mistress of tact, asked out of the blue. Josie refilled her glass before replying.

"That, my dear, is what we'd all like to know; except, maybe it's better if we don't." Then she was crying. Pam put an arm around her and Jas, who had been watching in silence, put his hand in his pocket and produced a packet of cigarettes and a lighter. Jo broke the seal on the pack and lit up, raising her eyes to meet his in gratitude. He simply smiled and raised his glass saying: "I came prepared."

Pam looked on in confusion. She had never seen Josie smoking before and she suddenly felt invisible as she realised that she was not part of the scene that was unfolding. Josie reached out and took Jas's hand.

"Thank you." She was almost whispering. Jas raised her hand to his lips and kissed it lightly before releasing it.

"My pleasure." Their eyes remained locked until Big Joe came out of the house. He nodded to Pam and Jas.

"They've all gone now, little Jo, so I thought I might take you and Susie out for dinner, if your friends don't mind."

"No thanks, Dad. Take Susie. I'm not hungry and I'm not much company either." Joe was a little disappointed, but he accepted her decision.

"I don't want to leave you here alone." He said.

"We'll stay with her until you get back, won't we Jas?"

"Yes, of course we will, if Jo wants us to."

Josie nodded. "I'd like that."

At seven-thirty Pam announced that she would like to watch "Eastenders", so they went indoors and turned on the TV. Pam kicked off her shoes and stretched out on the sofa. Jas sat in an armchair. Horatio curled up in Rick's chair, and Josie reclined on the floor, Cleopatra style, with a large cushion beneath her elbow. She felt quite tipsy, but it was a good feeling. She was with her two best friends and they were going to look after her. They were babysitting. She found the notion funny and she giggled softly looking from one to the other. Pam had fallen asleep, but Jas was looking at her with amusement. He grinned when their eyes met.

"You're looking better."

Jo blushed. "Was I looking bad then?" she asked.

Jas was embarrassed. "No, I didn't mean that. I meant you're looking happier."

"Well, I suppose I must be then." She struggled to stand up. "I think I'm going to make coffee, if I can remember where I left the kitchen." She was giggling again.

At that moment, Horatio woke up. It was as if he associated the word "kitchen" with food. He jumped out of the chair and landed in front of Josie as she started to move towards the door. She promptly tripped over him. Jas leapt to his feet and caught her just before her head would have hit the coffee table. He helped her to her feet and held her steady.

"Are you OK? That could have been nasty."

Her head was swimming; the alcohol and the fall combining to leave her feeling shaky.

"Don't let go. I can't get my balance." She pleaded. Jas held her firmly, one arm encircling her waist and the other her shoulders.

"You'll be alright in a minute, Jo. I won't let you go." She looked up at him and her head cleared a little. She thought of Pam's comments about chocolate bars, full of eastern promise. She put her arm around his neck and found herself saying:

"Kiss me, Jas, please kiss me." Then she passed out and Jas lowered her gently to the floor, pulling the cushion into position under her head. Aware of movement behind him, Jas turned to see Pam, sitting up and watching him.

"So tell me, Prince Charming, if she hadn't passed out would you have kissed her?"

Jas shook his head. "I don't know, but I hope not."

Pam could not resist following it up.

"Why not? It's obvious you're interested."

He didn't bother to deny it; instead he looked down at Josie and said "She's tired, grieving and vulnerable; it wouldn't be right to take advantage."

"You forgot to mention married." Pam squeezed his shoulder as she got up to make coffee.

"Yeah, that too." He said.

Chapter Thirteen

Day after day, my life carries on,
Looking for something already long gone.

(From Josie's Journal –Cards for all Occasions)

Josie went back to work the next day nursing a serious hangover. She had little recollection of the previous evening, which was a blessing and neither Jas nor Pam made any reference to it other than to ask how she was feeling and if she was really ready to return to work. She got through the morning with the help of black coffee and paracetamol. At one o'clock, her father came and took her out to lunch. They went to The Crown. There was no sign of Rick today and Josie breathed a sigh of relief as they sat down with their drinks. Big Joe wasted no time in getting to the point.

"Life has to go on, love. You can't go on grieving forever."

"I know, Dad. I'm dealing with it."

"Not by crawling into a bottle I hope. You were in a bad way last night. You mustn't make a habit of it." Josie bristled.

"Do you think I don't know that? I was the one who had to deal with Lee's problems for years. Do you think I'd make the same mistakes? Last night was a one-off." Joe patted her hand.

"I'm glad to hear it. I don't want to lose you too. Now, what are you going to do about Rick?"

The question took her by surprise and she looked away as she replied. "I don't know what you mean."

Joe shook his head.

"I wasn't born yesterday. When a man is spending so much time out of the house and sleeping alone when he's home there has to be something wrong. You're different when he's at home. It's like you're walking on egg shells. Is he seeing someone else?"

Josie studied the beer mat under her Coke and bit her lower lip. "I think so. I don't know what I should do. I can't even think about it."

"How do you feel about him? Do you still love him?"

Josie hesitated before answering.

"I don't even know the answer to that anymore." She felt a sudden surge of relief as she said the words. "The first time, it hurt so much I thought I'd die." She saw Joe's surprise and continued. "Oh this isn't the first time; there have been several over the years. Only, this time's different I think."

"How is it different?"

Josie took a deep breath before putting into words the feelings she had been concealing, even from herself.

"It's been going on for a lot longer; maybe six months with the odd night off." She laughed bitterly as she remembered Rick's brief return to the marital bed a few weeks ago. "And there's another thing. I'm not hurting anymore; I'm just angry that he thinks he can mess me about like this."

"So what happens now?" Joe asked. "Will you confront him? Maybe get a divorce?"

Josie was shocked at the suggestion. She had never considered the possibility.

"I can't get a divorce, Dad. You know that. The Church doesn't allow divorce."

"It doesn't condone adultery either. At least it didn't when I used to practise."

The meals they had ordered arrived and they ate in silence.

*

Pam was almost bursting with excitement when Josie got back to *Jasuprint.* She handed Jo a cup of coffee.

"Now sit down, girl and pin your ears back; I've got some gossip for you."

Loving the drama, Pam perched on the edge of Jo's desk and lowered her voice, glancing at the door every so often to make sure they were alone.

"Just after you left with your dad, Jas had visitors." She confided. Jo was unimpressed.

"This is an office. He's a businessman. He often has visitors."

"Not like these." She paused for effect. "There was this beautiful, I mean really beautiful, Indian woman, mid-thirties I'd say, and a scruffy-looking lad of eighteen or so. Could have been her son, I suppose. Anyway, he, Jas that is, looked delighted to see them. All hugs and kisses, then he whisks them off into his office and shuts the door." She lowered her voice still further. "They're still in there. I buzzed him to see if they wanted coffee or anything but he said no. My God Jo, you should see her. She's so elegant, designer gear from top to toe!"

She finally paused for breath. Josie felt strangely deflated. Of course, Jas must know hundreds of people from his own community. They probably needed some printing done. So why did she find the news of this visit so disturbing? Seeing that Pam was expecting a response, she forced a grin.

"So have you tried listening at the door?"

Pam laughed at the suggestion and picked up a glass pretending she was about to do just that. Josie's computer beeped to let her know she had a new e-mail. She turned to her screen and opened the message. She glanced quickly at Pam who had now gone back to her own desk, and then read the message. It started with an image of a yellow smiley face, and continued:

Hope you had a nice lunch. Come and meet
my family but don't tell Pam who they are,
it'll be fun to keep her guessing!

88

Jas

Josie smiled to herself and deleted the message putting on a serious expression for Pam's benefit.

"I've been summoned by the boss."

Pam's curiosity was nearly choking her.

"Are you sure he doesn't want me as well?"

"I'm afraid not. Hey cheer up; maybe he's going to sack me." Jo managed to get out of the room before the chuckle escaped.

She knocked lightly, entered Jas's office, and was instantly struck by the beauty of the woman who stood by the window. Pam had not exaggerated for a change. The woman was tall and slim. Her long black hair was sleek and shiny and she wore it loose, cascading down her back and across her slender shoulders. She had an unblemished complexion, finely defined bone structure and a full and smiling mouth, the lips bearing a light covering of a dark red lip gloss that enhanced their natural colouring.

"Ah, here she is." Jas was saying, rising to perform the introductions. "Jo, this is my sister, Suki."

The woman moved towards Jo and offered her hand. Jo noticed that beneath the perfectly arched eyebrows Suki had the same chocolate brown eyes as her brother, but hers had been subtly enhanced with a fine line of kohl on the inside of the lower lid, a technique Jo admired, but had never been able to master. They shook hands.

"Such a pretty name, is it short for Josephine?" Suki asked.

"Yes, but nobody's called me that since I left school."

"I was sorry to hear about your brother. Jas tells me you were very close."

"Yes, we were. I wanted to thank you for helping me to find him that day. I meant to ask Jas for your address so I could write to you."

Suki smiled and Jo was even more aware of her resemblance to Jas.

"No need for that. I was glad I could help and I know what it's like to have a brother. They're very precious."

"That's enough of that!" said Jas, steering his sister away from Jo who now noticed the room's other occupant. The sullen faced youth was sitting in a corner playing a hand held game of some kind. He hadn't moved anything but his thumbs since Josie entered the room. Jas placed a hand on his shoulder and the boy looked up.

"This is my son, Rajinder."

Josie moved across to shake hands, but the boy just nodded and returned to his game. It wouldn't have been easy to identify him as Jas's son. There was little similarity between the two. He was of a heavier build than his father, without having the height. His skin tone was much lighter, and the eyes that registered such a lack of interest were blue-green. His hair was very short, but what remained of it showed traces of red dye. Josie realised with some surprise that he was of mixed-race.

"Nice to meet you, Rajinder." She said to the top of his head. He mumbled something by way of reply. Jas started to apologise but stopped in mid-sentence as he saw Josie lean over and speak into the lad's ear.

"You'll have to speak up, love. At my age I don't hear too well." Rajinder's head jerked upright and he scrutinised Josie and then grinned at her. This time he spoke clearly and offered his hand.

"Pleased to meet you." He said, and added as an afterthought "You're not all that old."

The grin had transformed his face, making him appear much more attractive. Josie shook his hand and he resumed his game. Turning her attention away from him, she saw Jas and Suki giving her a silent round of applause. She felt a little flustered, but pleased at the accolade.

"Would you like some coffee or tea?" she offered. Suki shook her head.

"No thanks. We really have to be going now. I'm due at the surgery at four and I've promised to drop Rajinder in Firton. I'm sure we'll see you again soon."

Josie left them and went back to her own office where Pam was waiting expectantly. She put a finger to her lips to indicate that she could not say anything. Pam's frustration was almost tangible. Five minutes later, the door opened and Suki appeared with Rajinder.

"Can you spare a minute, Jo? I know what a slave-driver your boss is."

Josie laughed and asked what she could do. Suki closed the door and then noticed Pam for the first time.

"You must be Pam. Can you keep a secret? If not I'll have to ask you to leave us alone."

Pam didn't know how to react but Josie intervened.

"I'd trust Pam with anything. What's the secret?"

Suki was writing furiously on the memo pad she had picked up from Josie's desk.

"This is our address, and my mobile number. We're having a surprise party for Jas on Saturday. Will you come? Both of you, of course. We'll be starting about eight o'clock." She handed the paper to Josie.

"What's the occasion?" asked Pam.

"It's his birthday. You will come, won't you? Bring your families if you like."

Pam and Josie both said that they would go and Suki and her nephew checked the corridor to make sure Jas was still in his office before leaving. Pam came round to Josie's desk and looked at the address.

"Barnt Green? They must be in the money. Oh, this should be so much fun. I wonder if he has any single friends. Hey, come to that I didn't realise he was married."

Josie laughed as she realised that Pam still didn't know who Suki was. She thought the joke had gone on for long enough.

"He's not, she's his sister."

Pam was a little disappointed that there was no intrigue.

The door opened again and this time Rajinder was alone. He looked a little sheepish as he spoke directly to Josie.

"My aunt thinks I left this here." He said, pulling his game console out of his pocket. "But really I wanted to tell you something important."

Josie was intrigued. "Go on." She said.

"It's her birthday too on Saturday; they're twins, only she doesn't ever think about herself. It's always Dad and me first. I just wanted to tell you that."

"Is it a special birthday?" asked Pam, never one to be discreet. "How old will they be?"

Rajinder turned to her and laughed.

"If I told you that they'd kill me." He hurried off to rejoin his aunt in the car park, leaving Pam and Jo with plenty to think about.

Chapter Fourteen

How many years have I crawled at his feet?
Now, I find out his betrayal's complete.
This must be the end; I can bear it no longer.
Lord, in your mercy, help me to be stronger!

(From Josie's Journal – Cards for all Occasions)

It was Big Joe's last night in Birmingham. He was leaving early on Thursday morning to catch the ferry from Portsmouth to Cherbourg. His home at Hauteville-sur-mer was a three-hour drive from the port. Josie was sorry that he had to go, but she understood that he had built a new life for himself, away from painful memories, and at least now he was back in her life. France wasn't so far away and she knew that she could call him or even visit him without too much difficulty. Susie promised that she would spend the summer in Hauteville and had already checked out the ferry crossings for the end of June when her exams would be over.

Rick came home for dinner and managed to be fairly civil to his father-in-law for a couple of hours before closeting himself in the study claiming he had to work. This arrangement suited everyone as it left Josie and Susie to relax with Joe. Three times during the evening, the phone rang, but when Josie answered it the caller hung up. Each time, the number was withheld. It was a nuisance, but no-one paid a great deal of attention. At ten o'clock Rick came into the living room with a face like thunder, his mobile phone in his hand.

"Bloody battery's dead and I didn't realise." He said. "I need your charger Susie, I left mine at work." Rick stood tapping his foot impatiently until she returned. He connected the phone and charger to the wall socket and within minutes, the phone was beeping its message tone. He was clearly very agitated as he checked the messages and seemed to have forgotten that the others were there watching him, albeit discreetly, as they continued their conversation. He made a call consisting of four words.

"I'm on my way." Then he picked up his keys from the coffee table and left the house without a word.

Susie looked at her mother. "I wonder what that's all about." She said. Big Joe was watching his daughter very closely as she replied with a strained laugh.

"Oh you know your father – Rick Anson 'international man of mystery'. Anyway, we have an early start in the morning so how about some hot chocolate and an early night?"

Later, when Josie was lying in the darkness unable to sleep she heard the muffled sound of her mobile, ringing deep in her bag on the dressing table. She got out of bed and crossed the room but the ringing stopped. The missed call was listed as a private number.

They were up at six; Joe needed to be on the road within the hour. Josie and Susie waved until the car was out of sight and then arm-in-arm went back indoors where they cried for a while, both feeling that the house felt sad and empty now. Horatio sat between them on the sofa pushing his head under Josie's hand from time to time, forcing her to stroke him.

"Well, I'm going back to bed. I don't have to be in until ten." Susie announced. Josie pulled herself together and followed her daughter upstairs to get ready for work.

She arrived at the office at eight-fifteen. No-one else was in sight, but she could hear the sound of the machinery from the print room along the corridor churning out flyers and leaflets. Jas described these as "bread and butter" assignments because they provided the regular income on which the business depended. She set up the coffee maker and sat at her desk checking her email.

Her mobile rang; the call was from a private number. No-one spoke when she answered it, but she could hear muffled conversation. The voices moved closer to the phone and now she could recognise one of them. She listened, after all, it wasn't eavesdropping; someone had dialled her number.

"I've got to go now, babe." He was saying. "I'm late as it is." The sound of a kiss followed. "I'll pick you up at two."

"You're coming with me? Oh Rick, thank you."

"No need for thanks; I want to see this scan as much as you do. I want to see what our baby looks like."

Josie heard the sound of another kiss and then the call ended abruptly.

They had been married for nearly two years and now her period was late. Josie was so excited. She hadn't told Rick yet. She didn't want to risk disappointing him. The home-testing kits weren't so reliable in those days, so she had made an appointment at the family planning clinic and was now waiting patiently for the nurse to return and give her the result. She knew in her heart that she was pregnant; she'd known for days. All the early symptoms that she'd read about were there: the tenderness in her breasts; the frequent need to pass water and the nausea that woke her up each day. Besides, she could already sense the presence of the child inside her, growing and filling her with a sense of overwhelming love. The nurse was smiling when she came in.

"Sorry to have kept you, Mrs Anson. I'm happy to say that your test is positive. Congratulations."

Rick had been delighted. Throughout the pregnancy, he had been gentle and attentive; nothing was too much trouble for him. It was as if fatherhood was all he'd ever wanted. He took her out to show off her condition even when she felt too big or too tired to be bothered. He had attended every ante-natal appointment with her, tracking the development of his child. He even told her that she had never been more beautiful than during those months. Susie was born in July and Josie and Rick were thrilled. Rick cradled his daughter tenderly and whispered to her "You're beautiful, and one day you'll have a little brother or sister." That was something Josie had not been able to provide, but now...

Now someone else was going to give Susie the brother or sister Rick had promised her. Josie buried her face in her hands and shook her head. She had no choice; she could not take him back now. As she put the phone down on her desk and hot tears pricked the back of her eyes, she knew that her marriage was over.

Chapter Fifteen

By the time Pam breezed in half an hour later Josie had recovered her composure and started work. She was trying to write a verse on a nautical theme to put in a card for a naval officer who was about to retire. It had been commissioned by his daughter who had supplied so much information that Josie scarcely knew where to begin. She went through the notes, highlighting passages with a fluorescent pen as she looked for inspiration. Finally, she threw down the pen and laughed aloud.

"There's enough here to write a book, never mind a greetings card! Apparently, he won the Falklands war single-handed. How's the art work going?"

Pam gave a wry grin as she turned her sketchpad towards Josie and then both women laughed almost hysterically as they looked at the drawing. It was a caricature that resembled a cross between Captain Bird's Eye and Admiral Nelson. In the background, Pam had added a crude drawing of Rod Stewart with a speech bubble bearing the words 'We are sailing....'

"I don't think that will be the final version, somehow." Pam said. "I was having a little trouble with the concept so I got carried away. I vote we take a break and then it's back to the drawing-board." Josie agreed readily. Over coffee, the conversation turned to Saturday's party. Pam asked what Josie would be wearing.

"I haven't a clue, Pam. I hadn't thought about it." She didn't really feel like going to a party at all, but she couldn't say that to Pam. "I'm not very good at social events. I hate dressing up and all that."

Pam was relentless. "I'll sort you out, don't worry. Will Rick be coming?"

"No. He's otherwise engaged." Josie's facade was beginning to slip and there was a sharp edge to her voice. Still Pam pressed on.

"Ring 'what's her name' and ask if there's a dress code. I'd hate to show myself up." She was persistent and eventually Josie agreed. Suki answered the call on the first ring and seemed pleased to hear from Josie. She said that the dress code would be smart casual.

"After all, it's a surprise for Jas so he won't be dressed up. Just wear whatever you're comfortable in. I'm so pleased you're coming; it will mean a lot to him."

Josie relayed the information to Pam who still thought they should go out at lunchtime to buy new outfits.

Jas put in an appearance at eleven o'clock. He had been closeted in his office all morning with the accountant and now he was in need of caffeine. He helped himself and then perched on the edge of Josie's desk to drink it.

"I need a favour, girls." He was grinning. "It's something I know you'll be very good at."

Both women were curious.

"Well, it's two favours really I suppose." He continued. Now they were even more interested. "It's my sister's birthday on Saturday and I don't know what to buy for her. Will you go shopping for me if I give you an extra half-hour at lunchtime?"

"Yes." said Pam immediately, winking at Josie. "What's the second favour?"

"I'd like you to make a special card for her." He looked directly at Josie who nodded and smiled.

"I'm sure we can manage that."

"Thanks. I knew I could depend on you." He took a brown leather wallet from his pocket and placed his credit card on the desk. He wrote his PIN on the memo pad and handed it to Josie. "Get something very special." He said.

Pam picked up the card and grinned at him.

"We'll do our best. How old is she going to be then?" There was no stopping Pam sometimes. Jas shook his head.

"Naughty, naughty Pam. It's rude to ask a lady's age and she'd kill me if I told you." He finished his coffee and went back to his own office.

The shopping trip was a great success. Despite Pam's personal preference for flamboyant fashions, she displayed excellent taste when it came to choosing a gift for Suki. She led Josie to a jeweller's shop in the Bullring and rapidly selected a fine gold necklace with a matching bracelet. It was presented in a black velvet-covered case lined with red silk. Josie congratulated her on her choice. She thought the gold would look perfect against Suki's dark skin. Having paid for it with Jas's card and obtained a receipt, they realised they still had an hour of their extended lunchtime left and Josie found herself being dragged off to try on dresses. Her protests fell on deaf ears and half an hour later they left the shop with their purchases and still enough time to pick up a sandwich for lunch.

Jas was out at a meeting when they returned to work and by the time he arrived back at three-thirty, they had also completed Suki's card. Pam's artwork was a beautifully executed abstract design in water colours. It was in shades of red and involved shapes that looked like clouds outlined in gold glitter. Josie's verse was printed inside.

'My Sister, My Friend'

Sharing our heritage, sharing our dreams
Sharing our bloodline, our plans and our schemes
Growing together throughout passing years
Sharing our sorrows and sharing our tears
Paths that diverge and yet run side by side
Sharing our laughter and sharing our pride
Sharing our losses and sharing our gains
When all else has vanished, the love still remains
Sharing life's journey – beginning to end
We're always together my sister, my friend.

Jas was overwhelmed when he saw their handiwork. He admired the jewellery and he looked at the card over and over again.

"I don't know what to say. This is so beautiful; she's going to love it. Thank you so much. Now, I want you to both have an early finish today; we need to get 'Admiral Nelson' finished tomorrow and I sense you've been struggling." He gestured towards Pam's sketch, which was still lying on Josie's desk. Pam was on her feet and into her coat in a flash.

"You're the boss, see you tomorrow." She picked up her shopping bags and left. Josie turned to her computer.

"Aren't you going home?" asked Jas, sitting down at Pam's desk. "I thought you'd be glad of the extra time."

"There's no rush. Susie has lectures until six today and I don't want to go back to an empty house just yet." She picked up the notes and her highlighter. Jas was studying her intently.

"What about your husband? Does he work late tonight?"

Josie's self-control finally snapped and anger took over.

"I don't know and I don't care anymore. If he never comes home again it will still be too soon for me." She was shaking with anger at Rick and blushing with embarrassment that she had blurted out her feelings this way. She stood up. "I'd better go. I can't concentrate anyway." Then Jas was beside her, his arm around her shoulders.

"Hey, I didn't mean to upset you. I'm sorry if I spoke out of turn. I should mind my own business."

"It's not your fault; I'm such an idiot. Can we forget about it please? I shouldn't have said anything."

Jas nodded his agreement.

"All forgotten," He said "but will you let me buy you a drink at least, to prove there's no hard feelings?"

A little reluctantly, Josie agreed to the suggestion. She felt that she had made a fool of herself and wanted nothing more than to escape further embarrassment, but at the same time, the last thing she wanted was to offend Jas or leave him feeling that he was in any way responsible for her distress. She gathered up her belongings and they walked across the road to The Crown.

It was quiet at this time of day, in between the lunchtime rush and the early evening crowd of office workers who called in for a drink on the way home. Ted served them to soft drinks and they sat down at a table near the door. Jas broke the ice.

"You handled my son very effectively yesterday, by the way. He can be so moody at times."

"He'll grow out of it. Susie's had her moments too. They have to 'test the water', you know; find out how far they can go before you give up on them." Jo was relieved that they were now talking about Jas's problems rather than hers.

"How did you get to be so wise? Is it a female thing?" Jas was teasing slightly. "If Suki wasn't there I don't know how I'd cope with him."

"Does he ever see his mother?" Josie asked. Jas hesitated before replying and for a moment, she thought she shouldn't have asked. "I'm sorry, I didn't mean to pry."

"No, it's OK. As I told you, she left us when he was little. She came to see him a few times, but when he was about ten the visits stopped. She changed her phone number and we couldn't contact her. I even hired someone to try and trace her, for Rajinder, you understand, her part in my life was over. Then, last year, we had a letter from her sister saying that she had died in a road accident and that was that."

"How sad. I expect Rajinder is still grieving in his own way."

"That's what Suki says, but I was never sure. Perhaps that sort of understanding can only come from a woman. I'm pretty useless as a parent I think." Jas finished his drink.

"I doubt that." Josie's phone started to ring and she took it out to answer it. "Rick," she said frostily "what can I do for you?"

Jas made a move to leave the table and give her some privacy, but she signalled for him to stay. He sat down again and watched her face as she listened. Her eyes narrowed and her lips became a hard thin line. Two spots of red appeared on her cheekbones. She looked furious. Jas could not hear what Rick was saying, but he heard clearly enough when Josie responded.

"Don't bother to lie to me, Rick. There is no meeting in Manchester or anywhere else tonight." She reached across the table, her eyes pleading for support and Jas took her hand as she continued. "I know there's someone else and I know she's pregnant. It's over Rick; stay with her. She needs you more than I do."

She was shaking as she ended the call. Jas moved closer and put his arms around her; she rested her head on his shoulder, surprised that there were no tears.

"So now you know." She said quietly.

"My poor little Jo." He whispered, holding her gently until the shaking subsided.

Chapter Sixteen

I'm sorry, my dear, but I have to say
That idol of yours has feet made of clay,
And though this is news that will break your heart
You have to grow up – and it's now you must start.

(From Josie's Journal – Cards for all Occasions)

"Is Dad coming home for dinner tonight?" Susie called from the kitchen. Josie was sitting in Rick's chair nursing the cat and pretending to watch Midlands Today on the TV. She blinked to clear her head. Sooner or later Susie would have to know the truth. She took a deep breath.

"Come and sit down, love. There's something you should know." It wasn't an easy conversation. Susie loved her father despite his faults. She knew nothing of his past infidelities, or of the physical and mental cruelty her mother had endured for years. The news that he would not be home because his mistress was pregnant came as a huge shock to her and she didn't want to believe it.

"You've got it wrong, Mum; you must have. Dad's not like that. He might be moody, but he loves us."

"I'm sure he still loves you, Susie, but he stopped loving me a long time ago. We have to accept this. He's with someone else now." Josie was surprised at how calm she felt.

"You could put up a fight. I bet you could win him back if you wanted to." Susie was crying. Josie hugged her.

"That's just it; I don't think I want to."

Susie was horrified.

"How can you say that after all the years you've been together? He's my Dad! I don't want to lose him."

"You haven't lost him, love, I have. He'll always be your Dad but you have to remember he's going to have another child, and that child will need him too. So will its mother." There was silence for a minute while Susie thought about this.

"Don't you hate her Mum? I hate her for doing this to us."

"No, I don't hate her. I don't even know her name. Right now all I feel for her is sympathy."

Susie sighed and went back to the kitchen to prepare dinner. Josie hugged Horatio until he protested and wriggled free.

Susie retired to her bedroom after dinner, and an evening of soaps and comedy repeats on the TV left Josie with plenty of time to think. Before going to bed she went into the study and switched on the computer. She had things to say to Rick but she did not want to talk to him so she wrote a long email. This way she could say her piece without interruption or reaction. She said she would not stand in his way. They should get divorced so that he could have his freedom to be with the new family he had started. She warned him that he should stay close to Susie and promised that she would never do anything to damage his relationship with his daughter. She asked him to collect his things while she was at work as she didn't want to see him yet and she ended the message with some advice:

'Treat her kindly, your new love; you're not easy to live with, and if she loves you as much as I once did she'll need all the help she can get. Josie.'

She re-read the message and sent it to his work email address where he would be sure to read it first thing in the morning. Switching off the computer and the lights, she made her way up to bed.

Lee was playing his guitar and singing an old Tom Paxton song - 'Ramblin' Boy'. Jo and her friends sat around joining in the chorus and admiring the boy's skill. At fourteen, he was a brilliant musician. He had taught himself to play the guitar and the banjo. He could play almost any sort of music, but he was at his best when he played old folk songs or bluegrass; he seemed to lose himself completely in it. Jo's friend Sarah leaned across and whispered to her.

"He's gorgeous, is he seeing anyone?" Jo laughed.

"He's too young for you! He's only fourteen."

"I know, but look at him!" Sarah was gazing at Lee with adoration. Jo followed her gaze and looked at her little brother. He really was beautiful, if you could say that about a boy. He had shoulder–length, black hair that was so smooth and shiny it reflected the candlelight when he moved his head in time with the music. His deep blue eyes sparkled with mischief and his slightly turned-up nose added to his boyish charm. As the song ended and everyone applauded, he flashed a smile, revealing perfect teeth which were blindingly white. Yes, Jo could see why Sarah couldn't take her eyes off him. He called her over and she took the seat beside him as he started to play a Bob Dylan classic, which they often sang together. Jo looked around and the room was empty now except for Lee. He put down the guitar and took her hands in his.

"Hey Sis, keep smiling." He said. "Better things are round the corner." She squeezed his hands.

"I'm losing everything," she said. "I miss you, Lee."

"What's to miss, Jo? I'm never far away."

The sound of the alarm clock dispelled the image and Josie awoke to start the first day of her life without Rick. She felt surprisingly positive about it. At least she wouldn't have to check whether everything she wanted to do met with his approval. That meant there would be no arguments about her going to the party on Saturday.

Susie was quiet during breakfast but just as Josie was leaving for work, she called her back.

"Mum, I don't want to be caught in the middle of all this, and I don't want to take sides. Is it OK if I phone Dad later on? I need to talk to him."

Josie hugged her. "Of course it's OK. I don't want to come between you and him. Call him whenever you like, just not while I'm around."

Jas was sitting on her desk with two cups of coffee waiting when she walked into the office. He nodded towards the window and said he had seen her turn into the car park. She accepted her coffee and sat down. A few minutes elapsed with neither of them saying anything while Josie busied herself with logging on and checking her email. Finally, Jas spoke.

"So, it's back to Captain Bird's Eye today then?"

"Or should it be the Ancient Mariner?" Josie laughed and picked up her notes.

"The choice is yours; you're the verse artist."

"Of course, but you're the boss. I just do as I'm told. " Jas stood up and looked at her, a mischievous grin lighting up his face.

"Then I order you to write a verse called 'Hello Sailor'!"

At that, Josie started giggling and Jas joined in, spilling his coffee in the process. Pam arrived to find them in fits of laughter with Jas kneeling on the floor cleaning up the mess.

"What have you got that I haven't Josie Anson?" she asked, as she threw her coat over the back of her chair. "How do you bring a man to his knees at this time in the morning?" Jas stood up and bowed gracefully to Jo, still laughing.

"If that will be all, ma'am, I have a business to run."

"Then go and run it. We've got work to do." Josie dismissed him. Jas headed for the door but turned back towards her.

"You know where I am if you need me."

As he closed the door to his office, Pam was staring at Josie.

"Are you still going to tell me you're just good friends? That was positively flirtatious, and you've got that handsome husband to go home to."

"Yes, we are just good friends. No, it wasn't flirtatious; we were having a laugh and last but not least my handsome husband is no longer in residence. Pam, if your jaw drops any further we'll be scraping it off the floor."

The rest of the morning was taken up with explanations and work. By lunchtime Pam was up to date with Josie's latest news and the design for the 'Admiral's' card was complete. The artwork depicted a distinguished and decorated officer disembarking from a warship. Pam had drawn the man from a service photograph provided by his family and the likeness was excellent. Inspired by the picture, Josie had finally come up with a verse that struck the right note, speaking of the honour of serving Queen and country and the well-earned right to a long and happy retirement.

Halfway through the afternoon, while they were catching up with more routine assignments Pam looked up from her sketchpad.

"Have you got any plans for Monday, Jo? I've just remembered it's May day." Josie had forgotten too. There had been so much to think about in the last week. "Let's have a barbecue at my house; the forecast's good." Josie was hesitant.

"I'm not sure, Pam. I need to..."

"You need to what? Check with Rick? I don't think so. Or maybe you're waiting for a better offer?" She nodded towards the door. "I could always invite him too."

"I don't know what you're talking about." Jo was rooting around in her desk drawer to conceal her blushes. Pam let out a cynical laugh.

"You're not fooling anyone, Jo. Anyway, where's the harm? You're virtually a single woman now. Why not have a bit of fun?"

Josie shook her head and tried to explain that she would never be able to regard herself as a single woman. As a catholic, she would remain married to Rick in the eyes of the Church for life, even when the marriage was legally dissolved. Any sexual relationship she entered into would be adulterous. Pam struggled to understand her reasoning, but it was beyond her.

"That's so unfair. Rick gets everything he wants and your reward for years of fidelity and suffering is that your church says you have to be a born-again virgin for the rest of your life? Where's the sense in that? Even criminals get time off for good behaviour."

Josie shrugged; she had never thought about it in such detail before, believing as she had that she and Rick would be together forever. She didn't want to think about it now either so she attempted to close the subject.

"I don't see it as such a big deal. Sex is highly overrated in my view. I can live without it. Shall we have coffee?"

"Did I hear coffee mentioned?" Jas was standing in the doorway and as Josie made for the kitchen area she wondered with embarrassment what else he had heard.

Chapter Seventeen

So, I find my heart begins to heal
Things I've dreamt of turn out to be real.

(From Josie's Journal – Cards for all Occasions)

On Saturday afternoon, Josie lay back in the bath, scooping up the lavender scented foam in her hands and building shapes with it like she had as a little girl. Susie was spending the weekend with a friend and Jo was enjoying the freedom of the house. Horatio had followed her into the bathroom and was sitting on the toilet seat watching her curiously, as she played with the bubbles. Jo blew on her hands and a cloud of white froth floated upwards and drifted towards the cat, coming to rest gently on his nose, causing him to sneeze. Highly offended, he jumped down and scurried out through the open door. Josie laughed.

"That'll teach you that a lady needs a bit of privacy!" she called after him. She stretched out, basking in the sheer luxury of having no-one to consider but herself for a change. Closing her eyes, she let her mind wander and enjoyed the sensation of the warm water wrapping itself around her body.

Rick had collected his clothes on Friday while she was at work, and this morning Josie had sorted through the bathroom cabinets and removed all traces of him. Two half-empty bottles of after-shave, his toothbrush, deodorant, hair gel and even his favourite towels were dumped unceremoniously into a bin liner and thrown out. She felt purged and now the bath was completing the cleansing process. She put him out of her mind and concentrated on happier thoughts. Pam was coming over at five so they could get ready for the surprise party.

Josie was preparing for her first school disco. She was thirteen. She argued with her mother because she wanted to wear make-up and Annie thought she was too young. In the end they reached a compromise and she was allowed to apply a little foundation to conceal the spots on her chin, and some natural coloured lipstick. Josie and her best friend Sarah felt so grown-up that night as they set off. They danced with boys, and at the end of the evening Josie's partner, a gawky lad called Tim, kissed her. It was a clumsy effort, with much bumping of noses, and neither of them enjoyed the experience very much. The following week in school they avoided each other like the plague, each afraid that the other might expect a repeat performance.

Josie laughed at the memory as she let the water out of the bath and closed the shower curtain. She stood up and turned on the shower to shampoo her hair.

"Well, there'll be no fumbled kisses tonight." She thought, as she watched the soapy water form a whirlpool before it disappeared down the drain. She closed her eyes as she tipped her head back beneath the shower spray and her thoughts drifted away again.

She was falling and couldn't stop but then his arms were around her and he was promising he wouldn't let her go. She felt secure and she looked into his chocolate bar eyes and..

"Oh God!" she stood upright and turned off the shower as the rest of the scene flooded back into her consciousness. "I asked him to kiss me! Oh dear God, what was I thinking?" She wrapped herself in a towel; wound another into a turban around her damp hair and ran downstairs to phone Pam.

"Why didn't you say anything?" She asked as soon as Pam picked up the phone. "It was four days ago and you never said a thing!"

"Jo, calm down. You're not making sense. What should I have said?"

Josie struggled to make herself coherent. "You didn't tell me I'd asked Jas to kiss me." She said at last.

Pam chuckled softly. "Oh, that. I was wondering if you'd remember eventually. You were well out of it."

"But why didn't you tell me? I feel such a fool."

"Jas thought you'd be embarrassed. He said we should pretend it never happened. Don't worry, he doesn't think any less of you and he didn't take you up on your offer."

"I know." Josie was feeling calmer. "I'm sure I'd have remembered if he had. Pam, I'll drive tonight. We won't need to get a taxi."

"Why the change of plan?"

"I'd have thought that was obvious. I really don't think I should drink. I can't handle it. See you later."

They were ready at last, or nearly so. Pam was wearing the dress she had bought on Thursday. It was made from black stretch velvet and clung to her curvy figure, leaving little to the imagination.

Josie was a little uncomfortable as she looked in the mirror. Pam had persuaded her to buy a dress that she would never have chosen for herself. She loved the colour; it was midnight blue, but she was not sure about the style. She rarely wore dresses, preferring the comfort of trousers and tunic tops for work and jeans or leggings at home. She felt very exposed wearing a dress that barely reached her knees, and was bound to ride up further if she sat down.

"Are you sure it's not too short?" Pam surveyed her critically and then smiled.

"Jo, you have great legs. Don't be ashamed of them." Jo's eyes travelled upwards and she frowned again. The top half of the dress seemed skimpier now, than it had in the shop. It was what Susie would have called a 'boob tube', leaving her shoulders bare except for its narrow shoulder straps. She peered more closely at her reflection.

"Oh no; you can see my bra straps!" she moaned. Pam laughed hysterically as Josie tried desperately to adjust the dress. "It's not funny, Pam. I can't go out like this."

"Why not? Everyone else does." said Pam. "OK, I give in. Try these." Reaching into her handbag, she produced a pair of clear plastic straps designed to clip onto a bra in place of the original ones. She helped her friend make the necessary adjustments. Finally, although still feeling self-conscious, Josie announced that she was ready.

The house that Jas shared with Suki and Rajinder was huge. Josie and Pam guessed it must have at least eight bedrooms and there were several very expensive-looking cars parked on the forecourt. Most of the windows were in darkness. As they tentatively approached the front door, Rajinder opened it and ushered them into a spacious entrance hall.

"Auntie's through there." He pointed to a door on the right. "I have to watch out for Dad; he'll be here any minute."

The room was softly lit and about thirty people stood around, chatting in hushed tones as they awaited Jas's arrival. Suki detached herself from the couple she was with and came over to greet the two women. She shook hands with Pam and hugged Josie as she accepted the flowers and card that they had brought for her.

"Who told you Jas or Raj? I'll kill them!" Josie laughed and told her that it had been both of them. A look of understanding passed across Suki's face.

"Ah, that explains the sudden improvement in my brother's choice of gifts" she said, touching the gold necklace she was wearing. "I'm guessing he enlisted your help."

The door burst open and Rajinder appeared.

"He's just parking the car. I'll bring him in." Silence fell and everyone turned expectantly towards the door. They heard the sound of the front door opening and Rajinder greeting his father rather too loudly, "Dad, I've been waiting for you." Then Jas's voice sounding surprised.

"That makes a pleasant change; you spend most of the time trying to avoid me."

"Come on Dad, in here." Rajinder threw open the door and led his father into the room where everyone started singing "Happy Birthday". Jas was taken aback. The surprise had worked perfectly and he was all smiles as he patted his son's shoulder and hugged Suki, before moving around the room to greet and thank people for coming.

Josie watched him move from group to group, shaking hands with his guests or sometimes hugging them. She recognised a few of Jas's business associates who called at the office from time to time, and a small group of men who were obviously old friends as they greeted him with handshakes and laughter. Suki introduced him to a chic young woman with short blonde hair and incredibly green eyes who kissed his cheek and smiled seductively, touching his arm constantly as they made small talk.

Eventually he came to where Pam and Josie were standing, a little apart from the others, as they did not really know anyone else. His smile lit up his handsome features and Josie suddenly felt a little breathless. He was wearing a white v-necked tee shirt and black jeans. She was beginning to understand Susie's initial reaction to him.

"Pam, Jo how nice of you to come. Suki thought of everything!"

Pam handed him the bottle of Jack Daniel's they had brought for him. The gift tag read 'Happy Birthday, Boss, from the workforce.' He laughed.

"How well you know me! Come on, I'll introduce you to some people I think you'll like." He led them to the group of men he had been talking to earlier and whom he now introduced as members of his cricket team.

They were a friendly bunch and very mixed in all respects. Their professions ranged from bricklaying to legal practice and their races and colours were varied too. Pam winked at Josie and the message was clear. She had found what she was looking for this evening – a choice of eligible male company. She made conversation easily and managed to be very girly and flirtatious. Josie was out of her depth and moved away after a few minutes to sit down on the sofa and try to blend into the background. Suki came and offered her a drink. She accepted a glass of Coke and sat back looking around the room and wondering why she had come.

Pam was now engrossed in conversation with a tall, attractive Jamaican man and all Josie could think about was how much she wanted a cigarette. No-one else was smoking, so she assumed she would have to go outside. She made her way around the edge of the room, trying to be invisible by not making eye contact with anyone. Suki was circulating, chatting to everyone in turn and Jas seemed to be deep in conversation with the blonde woman who was hanging on his every word and laughing a little too loudly.

Finally, she reached the patio doors, which were standing open and she stepped out into the garden. She glanced at her watch. She had been here two hours, but she couldn't leave without Pam, so she was stuck. She cast her eyes around the garden. It was beautifully laid out. There were little winding paths that made their way through flowerbeds; a tidy lawn and a fishpond.

Then she spotted what she had been looking for. About half way down the garden, to the right there was a gazebo, lit up by solar lanterns. She made her way towards it and as she approached, the distinctive aroma of tobacco wafted towards her. The smoker was inside the shelter, but there was a garden bench outside and an ashtray. Josie sat down and opened her bag to get her cigarettes. Then a voice from behind took her by surprise.

"So you do have some vices then?" Rajinder stepped out of the gazebo, cigarette in hand, and sat down beside her.

She could smell beer on his breath. "I thought you were some kind of superwoman or a saint or something."

Josie thought she sensed some hostility.

"Whatever gave you that impression?"

"The things I've heard." He looked towards the house then blanched as a familiar figure appeared in the doorway. "Oh, shit; he's coming this way. He hates me smoking." Realising that the boy couldn't get rid of his cigarette without his actions being visible to Jas, who was coming down the path towards them, Josie reached over and took it out of his hand. As Jas arrived within earshot, she was saying:

"Are you sure no-one will mind me smoking here, Rajinder?" His eyes signalled his gratitude to her as he played along.

"It's fine, really. Dad and Auntie have lots of friends who smoke. Oh, and please call me Raj, I prefer it." He stood up as his father joined them.

"OK, Raj. Thank you."

"I was wondering where you two had got to." Jas sat down beside Jo. "Has my son been looking after you?"

"Yes. He was kind enough to show me where I could indulge my vice."

Raj coloured slightly at the remark, but Jas didn't notice, he was too busy looking at Jo.

"Good lad." He said without turning his head. "Why don't you go and get yourself a drink?"

Raj turned away and went into the house. "Are you OK, Jo? I'm sorry I haven't had a chance to talk much so far."

"I'm fine. Pam's in her element with your cricketing friends. I sometimes wish I could be more like her." She put her cigarette into the ashtray and looked towards the house. There was music and dancing inside, but she didn't want to go back. "I'm sorry, Jas. I'm not much company and I'm keeping you away from your other guests."

Jas shook his head. "You just don't get it, do you Jo? You don't need to be like Pam; you're perfect just the way you are. As for company, I came looking for you because you're all the company I want right now. You're intelligent, witty, caring and you look drop-dead gorgeous in that dress."

Jo stared at him, speechless for a moment. Slowly it dawned on her that he was being serious and she smiled as he moved closer and put his arm around her shoulders. Tilting her head so that their eyes met, she repeated the request she had made earlier in the week and this time he obliged. The kiss was tender yet full of passion and Jo was aware of a thousand butterflies taking flight in her stomach. The sensation was so intense that she moaned with pleasure and wished it could last forever.

Finally, the sound of voices caused them to straighten up. Suki was calling for Jas. He took Josie's arm and led her back to the house whispering:

"Let's dance, and then I can carry on holding you."

Chapter Eighteen

Just before midnight, Josie arrived home. She was relieved that Pam had decided to go to a nightclub with her new friend Karl, leaving her to drive home alone. She needed some time to sort out what was going on inside her head. Not that the drive had helped much; she still didn't know what was happening. She reflected on the evening's events as she undressed and pulled on her pyjamas.

"You look drop-dead gorgeous in that dress." He'd said and then they had kissed and the world had exploded inside her heart and she hadn't understood how it could happen, or why, and she didn't even care just as long as the feeling didn't go away and leave her empty again.

"Let's dance and then I can carry on holding you." He'd said and they had danced and the touch of his hands on her back, through the fabric of her dress had electrified her, and she thought everyone else in the room could sense her excitement, and she didn't even care because it felt so good.

"Drive safely, Cinderella." he'd teased when she said that she wanted to be home before midnight and he had walked her to her car, and their goodnight kiss had been sweet and chaste because Suki and Raj had come out to say goodnight.

She had thought of a line from Shakespeare as she waved goodbye:

'O, wilt thou leave me so unsatisfied?' and she had said aloud the response 'What satisfaction canst thou have tonight?'[1]

"Or any other night come to think of it." She said as she slid beneath the duvet. She turned off the bedside lamp

---

[1] ' Romeo and Juliet' –Act 2 Sc2 (The Balcony Scene)

and closed her eyes, but sleep didn't come. She tried counting sheep and breathing deeply, but nothing worked. Eventually she sat up and turned the lamp back on. Opening the drawer of her bedside table, she took out her journal – a hardcover notebook, which she had entitled "Cards for all Occasions" in case Rick ever discovered it. The journal contained her random thoughts and feelings, usually recorded in verse. Tonight, her heart and head were too confused to write and she stared for a long time at a blank page. At two o'clock, she received a text message.

'I can't sleep for thinking about you. Jas x'

She replied with *'Neither can I. Jo x'*.

Then her phone rang. He enquired politely about her journey home. She said it had been fine. There was a moment of silence and then:

"Tonight was special, Jo. I want you to know that. It wasn't just the party atmosphere and all that."

"It was special." She agreed. "I've been trying to get my head around it all night."

"I haven't taken off my tee-shirt yet because it still smells of your perfume, and I haven't brushed my teeth in case it washes the taste of you from my lips."

Josie gasped, she wasn't sure she was ready for the intensity of such a declaration, so she made light of it.

"I hope you'll manage to do both before we meet again."

At the other end of the line, Jas laughed, realising what she was doing.

"Well done! If I promise to stop talking in clichés, can we have lunch together? I'll even change my shirt!"

With great difficulty, she declined the offer.

"It's Sunday, Jas. I'll be going to church in a few hours and then Susie will be home in the afternoon. I haven't seen her since Friday night."

"Yes, of course." He sounded disappointed and Jo desperately wanted to make things better.

"Pam's having a barbecue on Monday. She was going to invite you. You could come with me if you like." She could almost hear him smiling.

"I like." he said.

Josie let out a little cry as the cat jumped onto her stomach and then settled on the pillow which had once been Rick's.

"What was that? Are you alright?" Jas asked.

Josie was giggling as she replied.

"It's only Horatio; he's just jumped into bed with me."

"Some guys have all the luck." Jas teased. Josie was glad he couldn't see the blush which flooded her face.

"Oh Jas! Any minute now I'll be expecting heavy breathing."

Jas didn't hesitate; he panted heavily into the phone and soon neither of them could speak for laughing. Eventually the laughter subsided and he said.

"I suppose I should let you go to sleep."

Suddenly, Josie was deadly serious.

"What happened to us tonight Jas?" she asked. "What's going to happen next?"

"You lit a candle in my heart a long time ago, Jo, and when we kissed tonight it fanned the flame. Now, I'm on fire. What happens next is up to you. Personally, I'm going to take a cold shower or I'll never sleep again. Will you call me tomorrow, or should I say later today?"

"I will. Goodnight Jas."

"Goodnight Jo." The line remained open as neither of them hung up. Finally, Josie spoke again.

"Jas..."

"Still here."

"I love your clichés." This time she did hang up before he could reply, and within minutes, she was sound asleep.

*

Father Paul raised his hands and blessed the congregation then concluded:

"The Mass is ended, let us go in peace."

As Josie joined in the response "Thanks be to God", she was acutely aware that she had hardly heard a word of the service this morning. Her mind had been all over the place. She made her way to the exit, stopping on the way to drop a pound coin into the box labelled "St. Anthony". He had always been her favourite saint. Many people pray to him when something has been lost. Others believe he always answers prayers if you make a donation to help the poor. She didn't know what she wanted to pray for. She thought of a slogan she had once read.

'Of all the things I've lost, I miss my mind the most.' [2] She smiled as she heard the coin drop and her prayer consisted of a single word.

"Help!"

It was raining heavily, but she was halfway home before she remembered to put up her umbrella. Susie was back by the time she walked into the house. She talked non-stop about her weekend as she made a pot of tea for Josie and they sat at the kitchen table. There had been a party on Friday night and Susie kept repeating how great it had been. Josie sensed her daughter's excitement and recognised its all too familiar cause. Teasing, she asked the question Susie had been waiting for.

"What's his name, love?"

Susie giggled before replying.

"It's Rob. He's really nice Mum, you'd like him."

"When do I get to meet him?"

"Not yet, Mum. It may not come to anything. He's going to call me later. He's got tickets for a gig tonight and he's asked me to go."

"That's nice. I'm pleased for you." She wanted to say more; to warn Susie not to get carried away. It was only a

---

[2] Repeated by several people including Ozzie Osbourne, but originally by Mark Twain(1835-1910)

few weeks since she had finished with Peter and she might still be vulnerable. The memory of last night stopped her from continuing. What right did she have to offer advice when she scarcely knew what she was doing herself? How could a kiss have created so much excitement and confusion in a mature woman?

"Mum, you're miles away!" Susie's voice cut into her reverie. "I asked how your evening was. Did you enjoy the party?"

Josie stared into her teacup as she replied.

"Yes. It was fine." Then, realising that Susie wanted more information she added, "Pam went off to a night club with someone she met there."

"She left you on your own? That was a bit selfish, wasn't it?"

"I didn't mind, love, honestly. I had a good time."

"Well, I expect Jas took care of you. He's so nice." Josie didn't reply; she was sure that if she did she would end up blushing like a teenager and having to explain herself.

Chapter Nineteen

What's going on, here? How long will it last?
How can these feelings have happened so fast?
All this confusion – my head's in a whirl
I haven't felt this way, since I was a girl.

(From Josie's Journal – Cards for all Occasions)

Susie went out to meet Rob after lunch and Josie fell asleep on the sofa. The phone interrupted her dreams an hour later. She was still in a daze when she answered. Pam was suitably apologetic.

"I'm sorry I ran out on you last night, Jo, but it was too good a chance to miss. Karl's great; we had such a laugh."

"It's OK; I was just fine. Are you seeing him again?"

"He's coming to the barbecue tomorrow. I hope this rain's stopped by then. You're still coming aren't you?"

"Yes, of course." She paused before continuing. "Jas is coming too, if you don't mind." She heard Pam gasp with surprise before replying.

"I don't mind, I was going to ask him anyway but *someone* didn't seem too keen on the idea. Is there something you're not telling me? Oh, let me guess! He's coming along as your very good friend and nothing more." Josie took a deep breath. She had to talk to someone about this and Pam was her best friend.

"Not exactly. I mean, he's still my very good friend but he's coming to the barbecue as my ...er ... date, I suppose you'd call it."

At the other end of the line, Pam squealed with delight. Josie felt a surge of relief that she could at least go to Pam's with Jas without the need for any pretences.

"So, are you going to tell me how this came about, or am I going to have to come round and torture you until you do?"

"Oh please don't; I'm tortured enough." Josie then gave Pam an edited version of events. She admitted to a little flirting, some dancing and a kiss, but omitted the details of how it had made her feel, and she didn't mention the late night phone call. Pam was fascinated and pressed her for more.

"So how was it, the kissing? Is he good?"

"Pam! Allow me some privacy please." Pam wasn't giving up that easily.

"Just one word, Jo, one word to describe the kiss and I'll leave it at that."

Knowing she was not going to escape Pam's curiosity, Josie decided to end the conversation by giving her friend something to think about.

"OK, in one word it was ... orgasmic. See you tomorrow." She put the phone down and started to laugh. Her laughter echoed around the empty room and she stopped abruptly as she realised what a lonely sound it was. Her thoughts turned to the events of the last few weeks and she felt again the joy of being reunited with her father; the pain of losing Lee; her anger at Rick's latest betrayal and her confusion about Jas.

She thought about Susie - her little girl who was now so grown-up that she had nearly become a mother herself not so long ago. At this very moment, she was out with a new boyfriend. Maybe she'd marry him one day, or if not him-someone else. She would be eighteen in July and off to University in the autumn, leaving Josie to rattle around in this empty house alone and redundant. Forcing back the tears, which were welling up inside her, she picked up the phone to call her father. A woman with a French accent answered and said that he wasn't home.

"Can you tell him I called, please? I'm his daughter." The woman became quite excited at this news.

123

"La petite Jo? Really? I am Madeleine – your papa will have told you of me, non? I will tell him of course, and you will come to see us in the summer, yes?"

Josie didn't know what to say. It seemed that Madeleine was a feature in her father's life that he had neglected to mention. She ended the conversation as politely as she could and then gave way to the tears.

Everyone was leaving her and she didn't know what she was expected to do next. She had lived for her family, and now she no longer knew who or what she was. Her world was falling apart around her. Lee had died; Rick was out of her life; and Joe and Susie had lives that she didn't even know about.

Annie's voice sounded in her head. She was angry.
"Stop it, little Jo. Self-pity will get you nowhere."

The harsh words didn't help. Josie cried for a long time, loneliness and the sense of loss overwhelming her. When the crying stopped, her throat and chest hurt from sobbing and her head was aching.

It was five o'clock and Horatio was playing with his food bowl in the kitchen to let her know he was hungry. She dragged herself to her feet and went into the kitchen to feed him. Her mobile was still on the table, where she had left it at lunchtime. It had been set to 'silent' since she had arrived at the church this morning. A blue light was flashing, indicating that there were messages for her. There were two texts from Jas. The first, sent at one o'clock, was short and sweet.

Just woke up, still thinking of you x

The second, an hour later read:

Guessing you can't reply right now. Call me when you can talk. I'll be waiting. Xx

Cursing herself for not having checked earlier, she pressed the speed dial and rang him. He answered on the first ring.

"Jo, I thought ... I was afraid you'd had a change of heart."

"No, I just ... I ... my phone ... I'm sorry." She couldn't string the sentence together. Hearing his voice had started a new ache inside her, one she didn't understand. "Can you come over?" She managed at last. "I need you."

"I'll be there in twenty minutes."

Josie breathed a sigh of relief. He was on his way. He hadn't asked any questions. She had said she needed him and that was enough; he would be here soon. She ran upstairs to wash her face and brush her hair and, as an afterthought, she exchanged her baggy green sweatshirt for a blue blouse that she hadn't worn since Rick had told her it showed too much cleavage. She might be feeling awful, but she didn't want to look it.

She threw herself into his arms as soon as the front door was closed behind him and he smothered her face with little kisses, finally meeting her lips with a passion that set her spine tingling. When they eventually separated and looked at each other they both laughed. Jas put an arm around her and steered her towards the kitchen.

"Now, why don't we have a cup of coffee and you can tell me what's bothering you; unless you'd prefer an action replay?" He kissed her cheek and she pretended to be making a tough decision.

"We'll talk first, but don't give up on the replay."

Once they sat down in the living room with their coffee and she started to talk, Josie realised that there was really very little to tell. She had felt lonely and this had caused an outbreak of fear and self-pity. Now that Jas was with her, the loneliness had passed and the other feelings were back in perspective.

"I feel a bit of a fraud now, getting you to come rushing over here just because I needed company and my daughter has a date."

"Yeah, you could have called Pam, she lives nearer." Jas said with mock seriousness.

"I suppose I could, but she doesn't comfort me like you do."

"I'm glad to hear it; although how anyone can resist you I don't know." He put his arm around her and she felt his strength surrounding her as she snuggled up to him. They stayed that way for a long time, savouring the closeness; sometimes laughing as they talked about anything and everything. Eventually Josie even told him about her conversation with Pam. He looked at her curiously.

"My hearing must be going. Did you say orgasmic?"

Josie blushed and hid her face against his arm.

"I had to say something. She wouldn't let it rest. You know what Pam's like. It was the first thing that came into my head. I'm sorry." She was so flustered that Jas couldn't help laughing.

"Don't apologise. I think I can live with that description. Orgasmic. Wow! Can I have that in writing?" Before he could tease her anymore, they heard the front door open and by the time Susie walked into the room they had moved to opposite ends of the sofa. Susie kissed Jo and nodded to Jas.

"Hi, I'm glad Mum's had some company. I felt a bit guilty about leaving her alone tonight when I've been away most of the weekend. Anyone for coffee?"

She was obviously walking on air after her date and seemed completely at ease with the idea of Jas spending time with her mother. Josie allowed herself to exhale. Perhaps in time, she would be able to tell Susie the truth about her changed relationship with Jas; but not until she'd worked out exactly how to describe it.

Chapter Twenty

It was a hot day. The sun was shining without mercy as their guests arrived for the garden party. Susie was ten years old and wanted a 'grown-up' birthday, so they had invited her friends and their parents to the celebration. Josie had been baking cakes and snacks for days. This morning had been spent preparing a buffet and salads, sorting out garden furniture and shopping for drinks. She was already exhausted and far too hot for comfort. She tugged irritably at the sleeves of her sweater and looked with envy at the other mums who were dressed to suit the weather in skimpy summer tops and shorts.

"You could at least try to look as if you're enjoying yourself." Rick hissed at her as she handed him the cold beer he'd sent her for. "Whatever's the matter with you?"

"I'm so hot. I think I might pass out." She replied.

"Well why did you choose to wear that stupid thing?" She looked at him and saw that he didn't remember, or that he had chosen to forget. She wanted to show him the bruises on her arms; the ones that he had caused last night, but she didn't dare. She had found the hotel receipt in his pocket and challenged him about it and he had denied it, as usual. The double room had been all that was available and he had stayed there alone. She had cried and said she didn't believe him and he had been furious and shaken her until she had to believe. The marks of his fingers were still there beneath the sweater.

"When can we have the cake, Mummy?"

"Whenever you like darling, it's your day." She led Susie to the table and lit the candles. She fainted as the guests sang "Happy Birthday".

Opening her eyes at last, relieved that she was in bed and not stuck in the half-world of her dream, Jo turned on the lamp and tried to read. It was five o'clock and she didn't need to get up for hours. Jas was picking her up at three o'clock to go to Pam's, but she didn't want to go back to sleep. Sleep meant dreams, and too often dreams led to tears these days.

Susie was up early and the sun was shining, so at eight o'clock they decided to have breakfast in the garden. They talked about their plans for the day. Susie was seeing Rob again. He was borrowing his mother's car and they were going for a drive into the country. Josie suggested that they should take a picnic, but Susie laughed at the notion.

"Mum, that's such an old-fashioned idea. We'll probably find a nice pub and eat there. What are you going to do with yourself?"

Josie told her about Pam's barbecue, and even went so far as to mention that Jas was giving her a lift in case she wanted to have a drink. She watched her daughter's reaction and was pleased to see that once again Susie didn't show any sign of objection to the friendship.

"That's cool." She said. "I won't need to worry about you then, and you don't need to worry about me either."

That agreed; Susie went off to start getting ready, while Josie sat and watched Horatio bask in the early morning sun.

Rob called for Susie at ten o'clock. He was in the house for less than two minutes before she whisked him away, but it was long enough for Josie to decide that he was an improvement on Peter. He was quite tall and well built, with bleached blond hair and hazel eyes. He smiled readily and had a firm handshake. His eyes followed Susie around the room as she picked up her bag and hugged her mother. Josie felt that was a good sign. It showed the level of his interest. Once they had gone, she checked the forecast. It was set to be a fine day with temperatures climbing to the mid-twenties.

By two o'clock, every item in her wardrobe had been examined and found wanting in some way. Jas would be here in an hour and she was still in her bathrobe. She phoned Pam to find out what she would be wearing.

"Not a lot, love. It's too warm to dress up, besides I'll be cooking. Just relax, Jo, wear something comfortable. It's only my house, not Buckingham Palace."

The advice didn't help. Pam had so much confidence that she could wear anything and get away with it. Josie wasn't like that. Years of being told what she should wear had left her unable to decide for herself. Her thoughts returned to the garden party when she had passed out because of the heat and her inappropriate clothes. She opened the drawer where she kept what she called 'holiday clothes'; things she hadn't worn for years. She chose a short red skirt and a red and white striped halter-neck top. Rick had told her, five years ago, that she was too old to wear them, but as she looked at her reflection in the mirror she began to think he may have been wrong. Pam was right, she did have great legs; and as for the rest, well she may never be a super model, but she had curves in all the right places.

She decided against wearing too much makeup. On a hot day, everything would streak down her face, so she settled for a little lilac eye shadow and some clear, cherry-flavoured lip-gloss. Tying her hair into a loose ponytail, she cast a final glance in the mirror, grinning as she applied the "L'Aimant" perfume that she loved.

"Eat your heart out, Rick." She said.

The doorbell rang; it was three o'clock precisely. Jas looked at her with obvious approval.

"Oh, Jo; you look fabulous." He said as he held the car door open and she got in. "Don't ever wear that outfit to the office though."

"Why not?" She followed his gaze and realised that her skirt had ridden up and she was showing a lot of thigh.

"Because we'd never get any work done and I'd have to sack everyone else so we could be alone." Josie adjusted her skirt as Jas climbed into the car.

"Spoilsport!" he laughed.

It was a small party. Pam had invited her sister and brother-in-law, and her neighbours from either side. Karl, in a white tee-shirt, tennis shorts and a chef's hat, was firing up the barbecue when Jas and Josie arrived. He was obviously feeling quite at home. Pam greeted them with hugs and then dragged Josie into the kitchen, leaving Jas and Karl to their own devices.

"Well done you!" she said as soon as they were alone. "You look amazing, and the boss scrubs up well too."

They looked through the window and Josie had to admit that Jas certainly did 'scrub up well'. He was wearing close-fitting dark blue jeans and a pale blue short-sleeved shirt that was open at the neck. The colour and style of the shirt seemed to highlight both the rich brown of his skin and his athletic build. As she admired the view, Josie couldn't help remarking

"Thank God he isn't wearing shorts. If his legs look as good as the rest of him I'd be completely lost."

Pam laughed heartily. "Oh well, that answers my next question then. Obviously, you haven't."

It took Josie a minute to catch Pam's meaning, then she was shocked.

"No, of course I haven't! Good Lord, Pam you know me better than that."

Pam was enjoying herself, laughing at Jo's discomfort.

"Well, all I can say is, it's taken you long enough to admit you fancy him, so I suppose it'll take forever for you to lose your Catholic inhibitions altogether! Come on, girl, let's get out there and socialise."

The party ended early, as everyone had to work on Tuesday. Jas drove Josie home at nine o'clock and they both agreed it would be for the best if he didn't come in for coffee.

"If I came in, I'm not sure I could promise to leave." He said as he kissed her goodnight in the car.

"And I'm not sure I'd be strong enough to insist." She walked to the front door and turned to wave goodbye. He blew her a kiss and she went inside.

Susie was talking heatedly on the phone, and as Josie came into the living room, she hung up with some force. She had been crying and her face was streaked with mascara. Josie sat beside her and tried to hug her but Susie pulled away.

"Not now, Mum. Sometimes a cuddle isn't going to make it better you know." She was very angry and she clenched her fists as she tried to bring her emotions under control.

"What is it, love? Do you want to talk about it?"

"Not really, but I suppose I'll have to sooner or later. I've just been talking to Dad." She almost spat out the words. "I'd put it off for a few days, hoping things were going to change; pretending he was going to come back. But, I'd had such a great day and you weren't here when I got back so I phoned him and *she* answered his phone!" She took a deep breath before continuing. "Anyway, he came on the line and I didn't know what to say to him at first so I asked who *she* was, and he said her name was Jess, and I was so angry. I asked him if it was short for Jezebel."

She was crying and laughing at the same time and now she held out her arms for the cuddle she had resisted earlier. Josie held her and stroked her hair.

"That was clever of you; I bet he didn't like that!"

"He didn't say much about it, because I think she was still in the room, but I could tell he was cross. He wants me to meet her. He said I'd like her and then I said something really dreadful and he hung up."

She was still shaking, but the sobs were subsiding. She had hardly ever argued with her father during her almost eighteen years and she was finding it very difficult.

"What did you say?"

"I told him he could fuck off and take his bitch with him." Susie looked at her mother almost defiantly, not sure what to expect, but after the initial shock of hearing her use that kind of language, Josie laughed.

"Susie, darling, you're brilliant! I wish I could have seen his face; the lying, cheating bastard."

Now it was Susie's turn to be shocked.

"Mum! I didn't know you knew words like that."

"You ain't heard nothing yet!" Josie laughed bitterly. "By the time I've finished talking to your father the air will be blue around him."

"I thought you didn't want to speak to him."

"I didn't, but I do now."

Susie went to have a shower and Josie picked up the phone.

Chapter Twenty-one

How could I think I could ever be free?
Nothing is right for a person like me.
All that is good must come to an end,
Denying a lover means losing a friend.

(From Josie's Journal –Cards for all Occasions)

Josie was feeling invincible. She had no idea how long it would last, but she intended to make the most of her new strength. The phone call to Rick last night had been therapeutic. She had said things she should have said years ago. She had sworn to make things as difficult as she could for him and 'Jezebel', as she and Susie now called his partner. For the last few days she had been living in a daze, but now she was fully awake and on the warpath.

She felt guilty that until now she had not really considered the impact of the situation on Susie. She had been burying her head in the sand and acting like a teenager; letting Jas kiss away her pain while her daughter was suffering in silence. It was all Rick's fault and she would make him pay.

"Think about what you've done to Susie!" she had yelled at him. "You've shattered her world." She had ended the conversation by saying that she couldn't possibly afford to initiate divorce proceedings so he was going to have a long wait before he could remarry. She had heard the surprise and frustration in his voice as he said:

"But Josie ..."

She hung up before he could finish the sentence.

Now she was unlocking the office, ready to start the first day of the rest of her life. There was no sign of Jas or Pam yet, so she powered up the computers and set the coffee maker into motion before settling at her desk to read her email. There was a message from Rick's work address. She was about to open it when Jas came in, 'suited and booted' as he always was for work, but minus the hair gel. He didn't use it at the weekend and she had told him yesterday that he looked better without it. He came over to her desk and kissed the back of her neck. She turned her face towards him and their lips met briefly. Jas's brow creased slightly.

"Is something wrong, Jo?"

She pointed out the email she had yet to open.

Jas squeezed her shoulder. "I'll go away and let you read it in peace."

"No, don't go." She opened the message and they read it together.

Josie,

Whatever you say or think I will find a way to marry Jess before my child is born. It's the son you wouldn't give me. You say you can't afford the legal fees – well get a bank loan or ask your 'nice kind boss' for a pay rise. If not, I'll have to start proceedings against you. I'm sure I'll find grounds. You can't pretend I was your one and only. What will Susie think of her Mummy when it all comes out in the open?

Rick.

By the time she had finished reading, Josie was in tears and Jas was rocking her gently in his arms.

"Take no notice, sweetheart. That's just the raving of a madman. He can't get his own way, so he wants to hurt you and frighten you into submission."

"I know that. I've lived with it for twenty years. Perhaps I should just do it his way after all." She dried her eyes. "Sorry, I'm always crying and laying my problems on you. You must get fed up with it."

"Not at all, I just wish I could wave a magic wand and make everything right for you."

Pam's arrival put an end to the conversation. She breezed in and threw her bag under her desk.

"Good morning, campers!" She said as she poured herself a cup of coffee and sat down. "What a great weekend it was. How are you two 'young' lovers?" She was teasing, but alarm bells started to ring in Josie's head. She looked at Jas, but he was one step ahead of her.

"Pam, we're not lovers, just very close friends. Have you ever heard that careless talk costs lives? Please don't make remarks that could impugn Jo's reputation. She's still a married woman."

Jo smiled her gratitude and Jas went to his office. After a while, Pam asked if she had caused offence and Josie showed her Rick's email.

"Jas is protecting me. We can't give Rick any ammunition; besides, we're not lovers yet."

"I see. Well you can rely on me not to say anything Jo, but that little word speaks volumes."

Josie blushed as she realised exactly what she had said.

The day was busy. Word was spreading rapidly about the bespoke greetings cards and there were five enquiries waiting. Two weddings, an eighteenth birthday, a christening and one, which made everyone laugh – *"Congratulations on your Divorce"*. Josie made the calls to get the background information. She passed it to Pam who started on the art work. They decided to start on the eighteenth birthday card; the other topics being a little too hot to handle today. Jas popped in, from time to time, on routine matters or to get coffee, but he was being so careful of Josie's reputation that he didn't even look at her when he spoke.

By two o'clock, Pam was fed up with the tension and when Jas came in with another enquiry slip, she stood up, saying:

"I need to get some new pencils Jas, is it OK if I slip out for half an hour?"

"Haven't we got any in stock?" He asked, studying the sketch she had been working on. She winked at Josie.

"Not the right kind for this project."

"Go on then, and don't forget to get a receipt for petty cash." When she had gone, closing the door behind her, Josie laughed and Jas looked at her with curiosity.

"What's so funny?"

"That was Pam's attempt at subtlety. There's nothing wrong with her pencils. She's trying to give us a bit of space without 'impugning my reputation'."

"Oh! I can be a bit dense sometimes. So, now that we're alone, would it be in order for two very close friends, who are definitely not lovers, to kiss?"

Josie got up and moved towards him, slowly as if she was considering the question.

"Well, I suppose it would be fine as long as the kiss wasn't too ..."

"Long or passionate?" He guessed.

She was standing in front of him now and she put her arms around his neck and drew him towards her.

"Orgasmic was the word I was looking for." She kissed him lightly at first, but when his arms went around her waist and his mouth responded to hers, she was aware of all sorts of new sensations coursing through her body, creating an almost unbearable longing inside her. As the kiss ended, she was sure that it had almost broken the rule.

"If I didn't know better," She said. "I'd swear you were trying to make a dishonest woman of me."

"Chance would be a fine thing, fair maiden. I think we should have some coffee and open that door, before anyone from the print room starts to get ideas." He made the drinks while Josie opened the door and returned to her seat at the computer. After a few minutes, he broke the silence which lay heavily between them.

"We have to be very careful, Jo. I don't want to see you hurt anymore."

"I know, but I hate all the pretence it's going to involve."

"It doesn't have to be that way. If you divorce Rick he'll leave you alone. I could pay your legal fees."

Josie stared at him and then exploded.

"And how would that look to the world? In order to save my honour, my very close friend (who is definitely not my lover) pays for my divorce so that my husband won't investigate our friendship and we can carry on being very close friends, but definitely not lovers. Or would that have to change because I'd owe you something? Just how long would it be, after buying my freedom, before you'd expect me to return the favour in kind by having sex with you?"

Jas was shocked and obviously hurt by this outburst. He shook his head and walked out of the room as he replied.

"You've got it all wrong, Jo. I don't want to have sex with you. I never wanted that."

Across the corridor, Jas closed his door.

Chapter Twenty-Two

It was nearly midnight and Rick was furious when the doorbell woke them. He refused to answer it.

"It'll be Lee again." He moaned. "He's the only person who'd have the gall to appear at this time of night. You go and sort him out. He's your brother!" Rick was right, of course. Josie let him in, guiding him to the sofa. He didn't seem to have much control over his limbs and his eyes had a faraway glazed look that Josie knew only too well.

There was no point asking him why he was here at this time of night. He wouldn't remember what had prompted the visit. He probably had no idea that it was late. When he got into this state it was a miracle that he remembered how to get here let alone why he had come.

She watched as he took out his cigarettes and fumbled unsuccessfully with the packet before giving up and falling asleep. She covered him with a blanket and curled up in the armchair, afraid to go back to bed and leave him alone. The last time he had stayed overnight, he had flooded the kitchen trying to make a cup of tea and he had made short work of Rick's bottle of 12-year-old malt whisky. She couldn't allow that to happen again. At all cost,s she had to keep the peace. Lee opened his eyes and for a moment, she thought he could see into her heart.

"Keep the peace, Sis. Don't rock the boat. Pour oil on troubled waters. Don't you just love clichés?" He closed his eyes again and...

Josie woke up to the sound of her message tone. She turned on the lamp and read the message.

Can I call you? Jas x

It was nearly midnight and she had been in bed for hours, crying, sleeping, dreaming and crying once more. She read the message again. Why did he want to call her? She had been completely out of order when he had tried to help her. She had seen the hurt in his eyes as he turned away from her, and she'd got it wrong. He didn't want to have sex with her. So that was OK wasn't it? Then why did she feel so wretched? More than anything else, she realised that she didn't want to lose his friendship and she hoped it wasn't too late. She sent the reply:

Yes please! Jo x

"I'm so sorry." She said as soon as he rang. "I don't know what came over me. Are we still friends?" She realised that she sounded rather pathetic, but she couldn't help it. She felt pathetic at the moment. She could hear something like relief in Jas's voice as he reassured her.

"Of course we are. Even best friends can have the odd misunderstanding now and then. I was worried about you, Jo. You've been through so much lately it's no wonder you feel threatened by everything. Are you OK?"

"I've got a lousy headache and sore eyes from crying, a stiff neck because I fell asleep sitting upright and I'm emotionally drained, but apart from that I'm fine." She tried to laugh, but the sound was thin and fragile. Jas's voice was soft and comforting.

"My poor darling..." he stopped himself. "Do you mind if I call you that?" Josie was cheering up a little.

"Actually, I rather like it."

"Why don't you have a few days off? You could use a proper rest. I know your boss will be sympathetic; he's a nice guy." Josie managed a proper laugh this time.

"Oh yeah, he's the best, but I have a problem with taking time off work."

"Really, why's that?"

"I'd miss my boss too much, and right now he's the best medicine I know." She paused to rub her aching neck. "I wish you were here, Jas."

"So do I. We'll just have to pretend. Let me make your headache better."

139

"How are you going to do that?" She was curious.

"Close your eyes and do as I say." He said softly; Jo couldn't stop a little laugh escaping.

"Now where have I heard that before?"

"Trust me, Jo. It'll help. Are you comfortable?"

"Apart from the pain, you mean? Yes. I'm sitting up in bed with lots of pillows at my back and my eyes are closed."

"That's good. I'm going to give you a psychic massage to take the pain away. But you have to help a little, so don't laugh!" He sounded very serious so she stifled her instinct to giggle. When he spoke again his voice seemed softer and smoother like rich dark chocolate.

"Relax, and imagine that I am your pillows, and then think of my hands on your shoulders." She found this surprisingly easy to do. "Now feel the gentle pressure of my thumbs working the tension away from your neck. Can you feel it, Jo?"

"I think so." She was starting to enjoy this. "Go on."

"Think of the scent of lavender and roses. Those are the oils I've chosen for you."

Josie was sure she could smell the combination of scents he had described and she sank back into the pillows and breathed deeply as he continued. "You can feel your muscles relaxing, as I work the oils into your neck and shoulders; the relaxation is spreading through your body." She sighed in agreement. "The pain is easing away now; you can feel it running out of you and your headache is clearing. It's almost gone now, hasn't it?" Jo could barely speak. She could feel his hands gently massaging away her aches and pains and the weariness she had felt all evening was leaving her.

"Yes. It's almost gone."

"One last thing," he said, as she listened carefully. "Imagine that we're together and my arms are around you. Now, please allow me to end your psychic massage by collecting my fee, which is a kiss."

"How do I deliver it?" Jo had really entered into the spirit of the activity now and wanted to continue.

"It's your turn to talk to me now."

"I'll try. Are you comfortable? Tell me where you are."

"My body is lying on my bed, comfortable and relaxed, but in my mind I'm holding you in my arms."

"We're holding each other and it feels good and we're happy; you are happy aren't you, Jas?"

"I'm very happy."

"I'm going give you a psychic kiss now. I'm looking into your eyes, you're looking into mine, and we're moving closer together. Now our lips are meeting and I can feel a tingle running down my spine as we kiss. I want you to feel it too. Can you sense my lips on yours and my hands caressing your back? Does it make your spine tingle?"

At the other end of the line, Jas whispered.

"It makes everything tingle. Oh you're so good at this." They were both silent for a moment before Josie spoke.

"My headache's gone. Thank you. Where did you learn to do that?"

Jas didn't answer at first, so she asked again.

"I picked it up from an Irish gypsy girl, many years ago." He said eventually. Jo laughed at his reticence. "I didn't want to tell you in case it upset you."

"How could I be upset by the fact that you've lived a little? You know so much of my life story and I know very little of yours. Tell me about her."

"There's not a lot to tell. I was twenty-two, she was eighteen. Her name was Kathleen. She had wild red hair and an even wilder attitude to life. We fell madly in lust; it wasn't love although we thought it was at the time. It was all about physical gratification and there was a lot of that for a while, but somehow we'd forgotten that sex can lead to complications. She became pregnant and I was delighted but she wasn't happy about it. Our son was born and she never really came to terms with motherhood. We realised, after a couple of years, that we'd fallen out of lust and had never been in love. She stayed on until Raj was five years old. You know the rest of the story."

"How did you feel when she left?"

"I'm ashamed to say, I felt relieved. There was nothing left of the initial attraction and I'd grown to hate the way she neglected our son, leaving Suki to do all the things a mother should do. Raj missed her a lot. He could only remember the good times, when she'd sing to him and tell him amazing stories. She had a gift for that, and a powerful imagination. It was reality and truth that she struggled with."

"Did you divorce her after she left?"

"It wasn't necessary. We were never legally married. It was all very 'new-age'; we had our own ceremony with a few friends, under some trees in the Lickey Hills, of all places. Suki thought we were crazy. It was the only time I ever came close to arguing with her. She thought we should do it 'properly', because of the baby, but I couldn't see the point. Kath and I weren't religious or anything and conventions didn't bother us."

There was a short silence as Jo tried to picture a younger Jas and his wild gypsy.

"I wish I could thank her." She said at last. "She passed on some amazing skills."

Jas laughed at this.

"Yes, I suppose she did, but you certainly caught on quickly for a beginner!"

Josie yawned, relaxed and sleepy now, yet reluctant to say goodnight. She found herself wishing that she could fall asleep in his arms. It would be so comforting and safe, because he didn't want to have sex with her. Suddenly, she sat bolt upright.

"Jas, there's something I've got to ask you, but I don't want any misunderstandings and I don't know how to say it."

"Just go for it Jo, and if I don't understand I can ask questions, right?"

"Why did you say you don't want to have sex with me? I mean, I'm not saying I want to, or anything like that, but aren't you attracted to me that way?" Her obvious confusion made him laugh gently.

"You still don't realise how much you mean to me! Of course, I'm attracted to you in every conceivable way. I hope that in time, you'll be able to feel the same way about me. When that day comes, I'll be waiting, and then we'll make love. It won't be 'having sex' because that's just about physical satisfaction and you're worth so much more to me than that. You're calling the shots, darling; nothing happens unless and until it's what you want."

"Thank you. That makes me feel better. I'm going to sleep now. Goodnight."

"Sweet dreams, Jo. See you tomorrow."

Chapter Twenty-Three

It's my turn now – revenge tastes sweet
Humiliation will be complete.

(From Josie's Journal – Cards for all Occasions)

When Susie came downstairs on Wednesday morning, she was surprised to see her mother already showered and dressed for work.

"You look much better today, Mum. I was really worried last night, when you went to bed so early. I was sure you'd have today off."

Josie handed her a cup of tea and some toast.

"I'm fine today, love. It was just a migraine, I think. I'd only get bored at home." She fiddled absent-mindedly with her rings and then took them off and placed them on the table. Susie studied her expression carefully.

"Dad rang me last night, after you'd gone up," she said. "He wants me to 'persuade you to co-operate'."

"Meaning what exactly?"

"Go ahead with a divorce, I guess, so he can marry Jezebel. I told him to leave me out of it."

"But what do you think I should do?"

"Seriously? Get rid of him, not for his convenience but for your own sake. He's my dad and I suppose part of me will always love him, but he's done wrong and he's hurt us and I think you should get him out of your life. He's going to suffer anyway – he's way too old to have a baby around!"

"Watch it, young lady; he's only two years older than I am!" Josie was trying to relieve Susie's anger.

"That's different. Besides, you wouldn't go off getting into that situation at your age. It's disgusting, and people say my generation has no self-control. Divorce him, Mum."

"I can't really afford to. It can cost a fortune."

144

Susie picked up Josie's engagement ring and studied it, then she laughed.

"I've just had the best idea! It would pay for the divorce and really annoy Dad."

"I like the sound of that; tell me about it."

"Sell your engagement ring. It's a proper diamond and 22 carat gold isn't it?" She was very excited, "But the best bit is, you don't sell it to a jeweller. You put it on e-bay and you email him the link. That way, he'll know that one way or another he will be paying for his freedom!"

They both laughed heartily at the idea. Rick was certainly going to hate this.

"Susie, you're priceless! Can you show me what to do?"

By the time Josie left for work, her ring was advertised on e-bay in a five-day auction with a reserve price of £1000. Josie had sent Rick an email link to the advert in a message confirming that she would look for a speedy divorce as soon as the sale went through.

On her way upstairs from the car park, she received a text message from Jas.

Fancy something hot and steamy before work? Coffee's on your desk! Xxxx

She was still grinning as she sat down and tasted the brew whilst sending her reply.

No sugar? Xxxx

"You're sweet enough already. Oh damn! There I go with those clichés again." He was standing in the doorway with his phone in his hand. "How are you today?"

He crossed the room and kissed her cheek, glancing behind him first to make sure they weren't observed.

"I'm fine thank you" She checked for observers and planted a light kiss on his lips. "Now, would you be so kind as to keep a respectful distance, before I get tempted to throw caution to the wind altogether?"

He walked round and sat at Pam's desk.

"Your wish is my command."

"I still love your clichés."

"That's as good a place to start as any, I suppose."

Pam arrived at that moment and Jas offered to make her coffee. She sat down, feigning shock, as he handed it to her.

"What's the catch? Who do you want me to kill? Or are you looking for the 'boss of the year award'?"

"So many questions, so little time! I'm off. The business won't run itself, you know." As he reached the door, Jo said:

"Two clichés for the price of one? Is that a special offer?"

Jas turned and grinned at her before leaving the room.

Later that morning, when Jas joined Josie and Pam for a coffee break, Josie received a phone call from Rick. He was livid. On impulse, Josie switched her phone to speaker mode so that they could all hear him.

"What the Hell are you playing at? I paid two grand for that ring. You've got no right to sell it."

"I have every right to do what I want with it and it's of no use to me anymore." She was enjoying his fury for a change. "I certainly don't want to wear it now."

"I'd have thought it might mean something to you," He sounded sulky. "If only for the memories."

"Yes, of course. I could wear it and remember that it signified years of broken promises. I could use it to remind me of the nights I spent alone, wondering whose bed you were sharing. Or maybe you'd have preferred me to give it back to you, and then you could have recycled it and given it to Jezebel. Would she have liked that, do you think?"

"Her name's *Jess,* short for *Jessica!*" He was yelling now, and for the first time Josie realised that she was actually getting to him. She was loving every minute.

"Is it? Well that's quite convenient. Her initial is the same as mine. Actually, you could have my wedding ring

146

back. Do you remember having our rings engraved with our initials '*R and J – together forever*'? I'll send it to you; it could save you some money. I just hope she realises that with you 'forever' has a sell-by date."

"You're such a bitch, Josie." He was running out of steam.

"Coming from a bastard like you, I'll take that as a compliment. My solicitor will be in touch when the e-bay auction closes." She ended the call, still shaking from the adrenalin rush it had caused.

Pam gave way to the laughter she had been stifling. "Jo, I didn't know you had it in you!"

Josie looked at Jas and he came over and put his arms around her.

"That took some doing. I'm so proud of you." Then, ignoring the fact that they were not alone, he kissed her.

"Oh, please. Get a room!" Pam said, still laughing. Blushing, Josie reluctantly pulled away from Jas and he let her go, with equal reluctance. Once he had gone back to his office Pam remarked: "You two are so good together it gives me goose bumps! I really hope things work out for you."

"I'm not really sure I know what that means." Josie was back at her computer, gazing at a blank screen.

"You still don't know what you want?"

"Oh, I know what I want alright; I just don't see how I can have it."

Inspiration struck and she started to work on the latest verse, thus ending any further discussion for a while.

At home that evening, Josie recounted the details of Rick's phone call to Susie who was more than satisfied with the result. They checked the progress of the ring on the internet and it was looking promising. With four days still to go, the latest bid was for £800. At this rate, it would certainly reach its reserve.

Later on, Rob came over to spend the evening with Susie. They sat with Josie for half an hour to be polite before disappearing up to Susie's room to watch a DVD. At a loose end, and not wanting to sit alone wondering what might be happening upstairs, Josie looked for something to occupy her mind.

Eventually, she went into the study and began to surf the internet to find out how to start divorce proceedings. It was something she knew nothing about. After visiting a few websites, she found what she wanted and was pleasantly surprised. It seemed that if a petition was uncontested, and the respondent was prepared to admit to adultery, the decree nisi could be issued in as little as sixteen weeks, and the decree absolute six weeks later. So, if she and Rick worked together he could be on his way down the aisle again in time for his forty-fifth birthday in mid-October.

She had decided that Susie was right. Getting Rick out of her life was the best thing she could do. It would leave him free to marry, but where would it leave her? Free to be seen with Jas in public, she supposed, but what about in private? A week ago, she had been so sure of her beliefs when she explained her stance on marriage, divorce and sex to Pam, but so much seemed to have changed since then. Not the teachings of the Church, of course; they remained constant and clear. Josie found that she could no longer see these things in black-and-white. So many shades of grey had become visible since her very close friend had kissed her for the first time on Saturday. She realised that she was walking a very fine line, and in truth, she wondered if she had already crossed it. Wasn't there something in St.Matthew about committing adultery in your heart?[3] If that were the case, wasn't she already as guilty as Rick?

---

[3] "You have heard that it was said, 'You shall not commit adultery.' But I say to you that anyone who looks at a woman with lust has already committed adultery with her in his heart."- Matthew 5:27-28

Logging off the computer, she went to the kitchen and made a cup of tea, which she took out into the garden. It was nine o'clock and getting quite dark. She looked up at the sky, but although she could vaguely make out the shape of the moon, she couldn't see a single star. Everything was masked by a veil of clouds. Her thoughts were like that. She closed her eyes.

"That's you, Sis." She could hear Lee's voice. She could almost see him pointing upwards. "You're somewhere behind the clouds, hiding away from it all."

"I don't know what you mean."

"You're making excuses, Sis. You're a grown-up woman and you're still waiting for someone to give you permission to play out. It's not going to happen. Don't be afraid to make a decision."

"What do you think I should do?"

*"It doesn't matter what you do, as long as **you** choose to do it."*

"I need time to think."

"Then take it, Jo. What's the hurry?" The image and the voice faded away and she opened her eyes again.

She went inside and phoned her father. Big Joe answered the phone and greeted her cheerfully. Before she had time to ask, he told her about Madeleine. She had been his 'life partner' for the last four years. He spoke of her with great affection and said he wanted, more than anything, for Josie to accept her. She was, he said, the comfort of his twilight years and he felt he had been blessed to find such a companion. Josie asked if they planned to marry, but the old man just laughed and said what would be the point, when they were happy as they were. She told him she was divorcing Rick and why.

"I'm so sorry it turned out that way, love." He said. "How are you coping?"

"Well enough, I suppose. I have Susie and my friends for support."

"Ah yes, Pam and Jas, what nice people."

"They're the best. Jas has been really good to me."

"That doesn't surprise me, little Jo. I've seen the way he looks at you."

"Oh." She didn't really know what to say.

"So does he stand a chance, now that Rick's off the scene?"

"I don't want to talk about it, Dad, not yet anyway."

"Enough said. Just one thing, though. It's time to look out for yourself now. Remember that. We'll talk soon."

"'Bye Dad, and give my regards to Madeleine."

"Thanks, love. I will."

Chapter Twenty-Four

*Goodbye, my love. While we're apart
I'll hold your image in my heart.*

(From Josie's Journal – Cards for all Occasions)

Later, as she was preparing for bed, Josie received a text message from Jas asking if she was free to talk. She called him. He was clearly in a flustered state and there seemed to be a lot of activity going on in the background.

"Jo, I need to talk to you, but not on the phone. I know it's late, but can we meet somewhere?"

Josie looked at the clock it was just after eleven and she was in her pyjamas. Still, he sounded so desperate.

"Can you come here?" she asked.

"What about Susie? Won't she think it's odd?"

"It *is* odd, Jas, but it would be even odder if I were to get dressed again and go out at this time of night. Besides, she's gone to bed."

He was there in fifteen minutes and Josie led him into the kitchen and offered him tea.

"What's it all about?" She said after they had embraced. "You look so stressed. It's not like you."

"I had to see you, but I haven't got much time. I have to leave for the airport in a few hours."

Josie's heart sank in her chest. Her first thought was that he was leaving her too.

"You're going away?" She felt her eyes filling with tears.

"Yes. My uncle has died and I have to go to Mumbai. He had no children of his own so it's up to me to organise his funeral and sort out his business affairs."

"I'm sorry, Jas. That's very sad." She took his hand. "Is there anything I can do?"

Jas shook his head.

"Just don't forget me while I'm away. I'll be gone for about a month. After the cremation I'll be making a pilgrimage to Varanasi to scatter his ashes in the Holy River, and then there'll be all the legal and financial stuff, as well as making sure his widow's cared for." He shook his head again as if trying to clear his thoughts. "I don't want to leave you, Jo. This is so hard for me."

"You have to go. We both know that, and I'll still be here when you get back. Perhaps a little time apart will do us good. Everything's happened so quickly; it's like being on a roller-coaster."

Jas looked at his watch and stood up.

"I've really got to go. I'll call you as often as I can, and email too. Raj is coming with me but Suki's staying here, so call her if there are any problems at work or anything, OK?" Josie nodded. They walked slowly to the door, putting off the parting for as long as possible.

In the hallway, they faced each other at last and kissed goodbye. As she closed the door behind him, Josie said a silent prayer that he would come back safely to her, and that she would know what to do when he did. Turning away from the door, she heard the sound of Susie's bedroom door closing. She thought nothing of it and after locking up and turning out the lights, she went to bed.

The next morning, Susie was in the kitchen when Josie came downstairs. She had clearly had a disturbed night and she wasted no time in getting to the point.

"Is there anything you want to tell me?" She asked.

"I don't think so, love." Josie had no idea what was going on. "Is there something you'd like to know?" She could see that Susie was struggling to control herself.

"What was Jas doing here so late last night?" Her tone was accusatory and Josie was aware of the likeness between Susie and Rick.

"He's been called away to India for a funeral. He came to say goodbye and leave instructions for work." She hoped that her face was not revealing the guilt she felt for the half-truth she was telling. "He was here for half an hour."

Susie looked as if she wanted to believe her mother, but there were clearly some doubts remaining.

"I was coming down to get a drink and I saw you in the hall, and I thought... well, you were wearing your pyjamas and you both looked kind of flustered. I thought about Dad and that woman, and I just went back to bed, but I didn't sleep much." Susie hugged her mother. "Tell me there's nothing going on, please."

Josie struggled to find a response that would not be an outright lie.

"Susie," she said at last. "Give me some credit. If I ever decided to get up to anything like that with Jas, or anyone else, I certainly wouldn't be wearing these pyjamas! They're hardly designed to inspire red-hot passion, are they?" She looked down at her ill-fitting, blue-checked pyjamas, buttoned up to the neck with trousers that were too long. They were old and faded, but they were comfortable. They also made her look completely shapeless. Susie looked too and they both laughed.

"You're right. He'd deserve more effort than that. I'm glad I was wrong, Mum. I didn't want you to be like Dad."

Josie was going to have a lot to think about over the next few weeks, and she wasn't looking forward to it.

Life at *Jasuprint* seemed strange without Jas. Pam was sympathetic, realising that Josie was feeling his absence more than she wanted to admit. She was still seeing Karl and by all accounts, they were having a wonderful time together. Karl was divorced and, like Pam, he was not looking for a serious relationship but wanted to have some fun. Josie tried to take an interest and even accepted an invitation to go out to dinner with them on one occasion. She didn't enjoy the evening very much because she couldn't stop thinking about Jas and envying Pam's freedom to spend time openly with

Karl. One good thing came out of the evening, however; Karl was a solicitor specialising in family law and he offered to handle Josie's divorce at a discounted rate.

The engagement ring sold for £1750 and as soon as the payment had cleared, Josie phoned Karl and the procedures were set in motion. There would be plenty of money to cover the legal fees and to pay for Susie's visit to her grandfather.

Jas had been gone for a week. He had phoned Josie twice but the calls were short and the reception poor. He emailed every day and it was in these messages that he was able to describe the details of his trip. He also told her how much he missed her and couldn't get her out of his mind. She read and re-read these messages when she got into work every morning.

Sometimes, he attached digital photos to the emails, showing the sights of Mumbai and more especially the rituals in Varanasi. The latest attachment was a photograph of Jas, bare-chested and dripping wet. It had been taken by Raj after they had followed the tradition of bathing in the Ganges. The lad was obviously very skilled with his high definition camera. He had captured the image perfectly with Jas smiling straight into the camera, and the droplets of water glistening on his face and torso. Looking at the picture, enlarged to fill the screen, Josie bit her lip and let out a little groan. Every day that he was away increased her longing for his return. Her replies were more prosaic than his messages. She felt inhibited and found it hard to express herself freely. The truth was that when it came to composing her replies, the verse artist had writer's block.

She didn't hear Pam come in, and was unaware of her presence until she heard her exclamation.

"Now that's what I call a work of art!" Pam was studying the photograph on Josie's monitor. "Look at that body!"

Embarrassed, Josie minimised the image.

154

"It's hard not to." She admitted. "He says he sent it in case I'd forgotten what he looked like – as if I could."

"You should send him one of you."

Josie protested that she wasn't photogenic; that she was sure he wouldn't want a picture of her and that if he saw her picture he wouldn't come back, but Pam was insistent. That evening she arrived at Josie's armed with her camera and took Josie upstairs for a makeover. She wore the midnight blue dress she had worn to the party, and at Pam's suggestion she wore her hair loose. It was a rich auburn colour and reached to her shoulders. Pam used a styling brush to create the kind of designer-tousled look that film stars often choose for public appearances. A little eye shadow and a very fine line of kohl inside the lower eyelid and Pam pronounced her handiwork ready.

Self-consciously, Josie looked at her reflection. She was pleased with the result and allowed Pam to take some photographs. When they went downstairs again, Susie was watching TV. She glanced up at her mother and then opened her eyes wide.

"Are you going out? You look great."

Pam replied.

"No, we were just taking photos for your mum's modelling portfolio. Now we have to email them to the agency." Pam was laughing. Susie raised an eyebrow.

"Oh well, whatever makes you happy." She said and returned to watching her programme as Josie and Pam went into the study to transfer the photos onto the computer. The 'photo shoot' had been fun, and Pam's constant teasing had created so much laughter that in almost all of the pictures Josie looked relaxed, happy and animated. In one particular shot, Pam had even managed to capture the sparkle in Josie's eyes. Pam said it made her look ten years younger and very sexy. This was the one which she decided to send to Jas. Pam went to make coffee so Josie could send her email in private. After a moment of thinking, she wrote:

155

Dear Jas,
Thank you for the photograph, the view was quite exotic,
As for comments on the pose? Well that was so erotic.
I envied every drop of water lying on your chest.
With images like that in mind, how is a girl to rest?

Now in return I'm sending you a photograph of me,
Although in mine I'm fully-clothed, as you can clearly see.
I made a little effort though, to that I must confess,
By putting on what has become my very favourite dress.
      Missing you,
            Love,
               Jo x

She had found it easier to write in verse than prose. It was also easier to use humour than try to express feelings that she wasn't yet prepared to acknowledge. She attached the JPEG file and sent the message, just as Pam returned.

"Have you done the deed?" She said, putting Josie's cup on the computer desk and settling into the basket-style chair, which was the only other seat in the small room.

"Yes. I don't suppose he'll see it until tomorrow. They're four and a half hours ahead of us, so that makes it half-past one there."

Pam laughed.

"You've got it all worked out, haven't you?"

Just then, the computer beeped as a new email arrived. It was a reply from Jas.

You're so beautiful, and if you're still at your computer, log in to Messenger and 'talk' to me!!!! Jas xxx

Pam read the message over her shoulder and said.

"Go on. I'll drink up and head for home."

Josie logged in and opened a conversation with Jas. They had never communicated with each other this way and now she wondered why they hadn't thought of it before. Pam left and soon Josie was engrossed in her online chat.

'Where did you get this idea from? It's great.' She typed.

'Thank the younger generation. Raj has been keeping in touch with his mates online since we left. He said I should try it. I loved the photo. I've made it the background on my laptop so I can look at you every time I use it.'

'That's nice, but won't someone else see it? Or does Raj use a different computer?'

'It doesn't matter if he sees it. He's pretty much guessed there's something between us anyway. Not that I've admitted to anything, but I won't lie to him if he asks.'

'Do you think he minds?'

'No. I think he quite likes the idea. We're getting on really well at the moment. We seem to have bonded on this trip.'

'So what has he said that makes you think he knows?'

'He keeps teasing me. He was doing it while he was taking that photo, telling me to think about you and smile, and asking if I thought you'd like it.'

'Tell him I did. See how he reacts to that. I don't mind him knowing we're close. If it weren't for Rick and Susie, I'd tell the world.'

'Is Susie a problem then?'

'Long story, but she's not in favour of me seeing anyone at the moment. I'll have to tread softly.'

'So that's how we describe it, seeing each other, I could never think of the right term. But right now I'm only seeing a photo and I miss you loads.'

'I miss you too. Hurry back.'

The conversation continued for a while and at the end, they had arranged to 'meet' online again the following evening.

Chapter Twenty-Five

Is this the total of my life —
Sister, Daughter, Mother, Wife?

(From Josie's Journal –Cards for all Occasions)

Over the next few days, Josie dropped hints to Susie that she may one day consider the possibility of dating again. Susie didn't want to discuss it, saying it was far too soon and anyway until the divorce came through it wasn't even possible. Josie gave up; she knew her place. Susie had exams to revise for that were due to start in just over a week. She also had her new boyfriend to occupy her thoughts, so she didn't have time to waste considering her mother's hypothetical future love life. For the time being, Jas would have to remain Josie's special secret.

In a way, Josie found it quite exciting conducting a relationship online each evening, minimising the conversation window if Susie came into the study while she was at the computer. Meanwhile in India, according to Jas, things were going much more easily. He had told his son that Josie had appreciated the photo and Raj had laughed and said:

"I knew you were going to send it to her."

Jas had then shown him Josie's picture on the laptop and Raj had given her the seal of approval.

"She's safe, Dad. I like her and she obviously makes you happy."

At least that was one less obstacle in their way, but Josie knew that the biggest obstacle of all was likely to be of her own making. When Jas left for India, she had hoped that the separation would help to clear her confusion; it hadn't. Instead, she had become even more concerned about their relationship because she realised that it went far deeper than she had originally thought.

Alone in the dark, before she went to sleep, she would find herself hugging her pillow and imagining it was him. She knew now that she had fallen in love with him and in some ways that was almost disastrous. Given her daughter's opposition and her own religious beliefs, it seemed as if there could never be a happy ending for her. She couldn't even tell Jas how she felt. She didn't think it would be fair to him to say that she loved him but they could never be together unless Susie changed her mind and the Catholic Church its teachings. True, he had never actually said that he loved her, but she was sure that he did, surer than she had ever been with Rick, even during the early days of their courtship and marriage.

Jas had now been away for exactly two weeks. Josie and Pam were sorting through the post at work when Suki arrived. As usual, she was a picture of elegance.

"Jas asked me to stop by and see how things were going." She said. "Is there anything you need?"

"I think we have everything under control." Said Pam. "But you could join us for coffee if you like while we finish sorting this lot."

Suki accepted the offer and spent the next half-hour helping out. Pam was very chatty and asked how Jas was getting on in India. Josie was quieter, feeling shy and awkward for reasons she didn't fully understand. After a while, Pam excused herself to take a piece of artwork to the print room and Suki surprised Josie by inviting her out to lunch.

"I think it would be good if we got to know each other a little better." She explained.

Josie accepted the invitation and they arranged to meet at Café Rouge at one o'clock. When Pam came back Suki left and work was resumed.

Suki was sitting at a table on the terrace and she rose to greet Josie.

"I thought you might prefer to be outside as I know you like a cigarette sometimes."

Josie thanked her and sat down. "I didn't think you'd approve of smoking." She said.

"Well, I can't really in my profession, but life's too short to deny ourselves everything we enjoy isn't it?"

Josie had the impression that Suki was not only talking about smoking. Suki watched as Josie lit a cigarette and inhaled. When she spoke again she was very direct.

"My brother is an exceptional man." She said. "We've always been very close. I know you understand exactly how that is. You won't do anything to hurt him will you?"

"How could I do that?" Josie was being cautious. She didn't know if Jas had spoken to Suki about their relationship.

"More easily than you realise, Jo. He hasn't discussed it with me, but I can guess what's happening. His eyes light up at the mention of your name, and I saw the way he looked at you at our party and the way you danced together. He's been different since that night. Did something happen?"

Josie could tell that there was no point trying to hide anything. She nodded and then raised her eyes to meet Suki's, which were so like Jas's, so beautiful you could drown in them.

"We kissed. It was the first time, but not the last. We've been in touch every day since he's been away."

"And when he comes back – what then?"

"I don't know. I have issues I need to resolve with myself before then."

The waitress brought their meals and when she had gone Suki continued her questioning until at last Josie opened up to her and poured out the contents of her heart and mind. In twenty minutes, she had revealed her life story as she saw it. She was fighting back tears as she ended by telling Suki about the conflict between her feelings for Jas, her loyalty to her daughter and her religious inhibitions. Suki studied her for a moment and then asked:

"Where do *you* fit into the picture? I'm hearing about your late brother, your father, your daughter, your Church and your husband. I'm even hearing about *my* brother and your concern for *his* feelings. I'm not hearing what *you* want."

"I don't understand."

"It seems to me that you've spent your whole life defining yourself by your relationships with other people. Sister, daughter, mother, and wife – these are your job titles. They're only what you do, not who you are. You even define yourself by your religion."

Josie looked at her in amazement, realising that Suki had somehow managed to sum her up in a few short sentences, and she was absolutely right.

"So what should I do now?" She asked.

"Take control, Jo, and even more important – lose the possessive pronoun. Stop thinking you're *his* daughter or *her* mother. The person that is "Josie" belongs to you alone and only you can redefine her."

At last, Josie began to see things in perspective. As they settled the bill and left the table, she hugged Suki.

"Thank you so much. You've helped me a lot."

Suki kissed her cheek and stroked her hair.

"I hope so, you're such a sweetheart I can see why Jas fell for you; it's the innocence and selflessness, but the time has come for you to be a little selfish."

After a seemingly endless afternoon at work, Josie was finally stretched out on the sofa at home. She was making resolutions. She would make her own decisions from now on. She would point out to Susie that she had the right to a life of her own. She would redefine herself as Suki had suggested. She would start as soon as Susie came home, but it wasn't that easy. When Susie came in at half-past six, Rob

161

was with her. He had picked her up from college and they went straight to Susie's room, so there would be no chance of Josie talking to her tonight.

Horatio climbed onto the arm of the sofa and looked at her with his head tilted to one side. Josie stroked him between his ears and he purred with satisfaction. She leaned towards him and he licked her chin.

"So what do you think Horatio? How does a woman redefine herself?" The cat started to groom himself. "Is that a hint? Do I need a new image?" She laughed. "Now I know I'm going crazy, asking a cat for advice." She got up and went into the study. Jas wouldn't be online for another hour but she could find some way to amuse herself. Since childhood, Josie had always done her best thinking in verse. Now she typed:

Redefining Josie

I look at my reflection, a woman in my prime.
At forty-three I realise that I have served my time.
Redundant as a sister, rejected as a wife
Perhaps the time has come for me to reassess my life?
Successful as a mother, but my child is fully grown
My father's many miles away with a lover of his own.
So what becomes of Josie in the years that lie ahead?
Must I keep the Faith and perish as I lie alone in bed?

There were still so many questions but so few answers. Jas appeared online and they had their nightly exchange. It was comforting to read his words, but she longed to hear his voice and see his face. She told him about having lunch with Suki, but didn't go into detail about their conversation. Instead, she cut and pasted the poem she had written earlier into the conversation.

'You don't ever need to be alone Jo. ' Jas typed when he had read it. *'Once I get back I'm never going to leave you again.'*

When they had signed off Josie went to bed with a mug of cocoa, calling out to say goodnight to Susie and Rob who hadn't been downstairs all evening.

Chapter Twenty-Six

Another week went by. Susie had started her exams and they were going well. Josie made sure that her daughter ate a good breakfast on the days when she had a paper, and was sure to ask all the right questions at the end of the day to show her support. She continued to 'talk' to Jas online each evening and she was looking forward to his return in a week.

There had been a few phone calls from Rick raging about her solicitor's financial proposals. He wanted the house, which they owned outright, but on Karl's advice, Josie was refusing to let him buy her out. Even if Rick were to give her half the market value in cash, she would struggle to be able to afford a mortgage on her own. He told her that she could rent a flat; after all, she would be on her own once Susie went away to University. He claimed that he needed the house more than she did, as he would soon have a new family to care for. Josie laughed at this and told him to talk to her solicitor.

Karl was brilliant in the way he handled Rick. He was completely unperturbed by the verbal aggression and threatening manner. He rang Josie one evening and could barely keep himself from laughing aloud.

"I've just spoken to Rick's solicitor." He said. "Apparently Rick wanted to claim that you'd been unfaithful before he was. He thought it might help his case with the financial settlement."

"He won't get anywhere with that. I've never been with another man."

"I know, and so does he now. Even his own solicitor asked him just how long he wanted this divorce to take. He's beginning to realise that if he wants it over quickly he's got to be prepared to give some ground. He's worth a fair bit in investments and so on, you know. We could go for half. You'd probably get it."

Josie thought for a moment before answering.

"Karl, you're doing a great job and I appreciate it, but I want this over quickly too. He's blighted my life for long enough. If he lets me keep the house I'll be happy."

"You're easily satisfied Jo, but you're probably right. That way you can get on with your own life. I'll put that to him tomorrow."

At last, the day came when Jas was due to come home. It was Friday 15th June, and the day was hot and sunny. Josie could barely contain her excitement at the prospect of seeing him again. She didn't expect to see him until Saturday, because she was sure he would be tired, but at least they could talk on the phone tonight. She and Pam were working and chatting in their usual fashion when the phone rang at eleven o'clock. It was Suki asking for Josie. Pam handed over the phone.

"Jo, can you do me an enormous favour? I was supposed to pick up Jas and Raj from the airport later, but my colleague has been called away and I have to cover his clinic. Will you do it for me?"

Josie agreed without hesitation. They were due to arrive on a Lufthansa flight at 12.45 from Frankfurt where they had changed planes. She put down the phone and grinned as she passed the news on to Pam. Then she groaned.

"Oh Lord. How do I look Pam? I wish I'd washed my hair this morning. I wasn't expecting to see him until tomorrow."

"I don't suppose he'll even notice because he'll be so surprised to see you too."

She arrived at the airport with fifteen minutes to spare and checked the details of the flight. It was due in on time. Suki had arranged with Jas that they would meet in the coffee bar in Terminal 1, as she didn't want to stand around waiting for them to collect their luggage, so Josie bought herself a cappuccino and settled down to wait. Eventually she saw them approaching from the arrivals gate and stood up to wave. Raj saw her first. He gave his father's arm a tug and pointed to her.

Jas stood still for a moment, smiling and then waved back as they hurried towards her and placed their suitcases on the floor.

There was an awkward moment when neither Jas nor Josie knew quite how to greet each other in a public place, in the presence of Jas's son. Josie broke the silence.

"Suki couldn't make it. She asked me to come and get you. Welcome back."

Jas smiled and took her hand.

"Thanks. It's good to be back."

Raj stood watching them and then he laughed.

"It's nice of you to be here Josie. Dad, don't you think you should kiss her or something? I'm sure she deserves more than a handshake."

"Rajinder!" Jas turned to reprimand his son, but Josie stopped him by putting her finger on his lips. Without taking her eyes from Jas she said:

"Raj, would you go and get me a newspaper please?"

"OK. Which one do you want?"

"Get whichever one you'd like to read while your father takes your advice." She moved closer to Jas who was laughing now as he put his arms around her.

"Take your time, son." He said to Raj who was still laughing as he left them locked in an embrace.

"It's so good to see you!" Jas said as they finally let go of each other and sat down. "It's seemed like forever. I've got so many things to tell you about. I wish you could have come with me. I missed you so much."

"I missed you too and I have things to tell you as well."

Raj strolled over to the table, making a great show of walking very slowly.

"Was I gone long enough?" He asked as he sat down. "Is the mushy stuff over?"

"It's over for the time being." Josie smiled at him. "Now, do you guys want coffee or shall I take you home?"

As they parked in the driveway, Suki's car pulled up behind them. She greeted her brother and nephew with great enthusiasm and affection, and then turned to thank Josie while Jas and Raj took their luggage inside.

"You'll stay for some tea of course." She said. It was not a question. She linked arms with Josie and led her into the house. "I hope you didn't mind my little subterfuge." She said confidentially. "I thought you might like to be there as soon as he arrived."

"There was no clinic?" Josie was laughing. "I didn't mind at all. Thank you."

Suki took her into an enormous kitchen, which boasted a cosy area furnished with two leather sofas and a large coffee table.

"Make yourself at home, Jo. The boys will join us when they've freshened up. We always take tea in here."

Josie sat down and looked around her. The last time she had been in the house, she had only seen the large lounge, the garden and the cloakroom. The kitchen had an atmosphere all of its own. At the far end, in the cooking area there were gleaming granite worktops, spacious cupboards an enormous fridge-freezer and an Aga, which Josie found quite daunting. In the central area, at the breakfast bar where Suki was making tea, there was a microwave, a kettle, a smaller fridge and more cupboards. Yet despite the grandeur, Josie felt quite at ease. This was obviously the hub of the household.

On the wall nearby there was a notice board with a random collection of receipts, invitations and notes attached to it. Underneath it a shelf was crammed with framed photographs. Josie got up to look at them. Her attention was immediately drawn to a picture of a little boy and girl in matching school uniforms of grey and red. They were holding hands and smiling broadly. It was in a beautiful dark wooden frame and the gold coloured plaque attached to it was engraved with the words:

Jaswant and Sukheshi start school
September 1972

Suki brought the tea tray and set it down on the coffee table.

"We were four years old in that one." Suki said. "Dad took that photo. He was so proud of us. He died when we were ten, and Mum shortly afterwards." She seemed far away in her thoughts.

"Who looked after you then?"

"Our legal guardian was Dad's sister, but we had a nanny who really brought us up. We've been very lucky. We've always had everything we needed, more than we need in fact."

Jas and Raj came into the kitchen. They had showered and changed out of their travelling clothes. Jas sat beside Josie and Raj sat with Suki on the other sofa. Josie felt so comfortable with this happy little family. Suki ruffled her nephew's hair.

"Well Raj, you seem to have grown up a bit while you've been away. It's good to see you treating your father with more respect." She said.

"I think we got to understand each other better. Didn't we Dad?" He said with more maturity than Josie had seen in him before.

"Yes. I think we did. I never knew you were so good with a camera for starters, or that you'd make such a good paper boy." He winked at his son who looked at Josie and the three of them laughed. Suki looked on in confusion.

"Is someone going to fill me in?" She asked.

"Not just yet." Jas stood up and looked down at Josie. "Right now, I'd like to show Jo the garden by daylight; she's only seen it in the dark." He took her hand and she got up and followed him out through the back door to the spot where they had first kissed. Once they were alone they relived the moment, and it was even sweeter.

Chapter Twenty-Seven

Josie arrived home just before Susie. It had been the day of Susie's last exam, so Josie had declined the invitation from Suki to stay and have dinner with the family. She had promised Jas that she would try to see him later on if all was well at home. She felt guilty that after a month apart she couldn't drop everything to spend time with him.

When Susie came in she said the exam had been fine and that she thought she'd done well. Then she announced that she was going out with Rob and she rushed upstairs to get ready. Josie stared after her for a moment. She was seldom angry with Susie, but on this occasion, she could feel resentment growing inside her. She had rushed home to be here for her daughter for the sake of five minutes. She thought of Suki telling her it was time for her to be a little selfish, and before she had time to change her mind she picked up her phone and called Jas.

"I'm free tonight." She said as soon as he answered. He suggested that they should go for a drive and find a nice country pub. Josie thought that would be perfect and arranged for him to pick her up in an hour.

Susie had just finished showering and was on her way across the landing, when Josie went upstairs.

"Oh good, I'm glad the bathroom's free. I've got to have a shower and get changed." She said.

"Are you going out then, Mum?" Susie seemed surprised.

It was now or never, Josie decided. She wasn't prepared to lie anymore.

"Yes. Jas is calling for me in an hour. We're going out for a drink."

Susie stared at her. "I thought he was in India."

"He came back today. I picked him up from the airport and he's taking me out tonight." Her tone was almost challenging.

"He's taking you out? So this is a date, is it?" Susie looked upset. "You can't do that."

"Susie, I can and I will. I don't need you or anyone to tell me what I can do. Anyway, I thought you liked Jas."

"I did, but that was before he wanted to date *my mother.*"

"Being your mother is not the only thing I am, Susie. Jas doesn't want your mother, he wants *me*; the person not the job description."

"Don't you like being a mother anymore? I thought you loved me." Susie's lower lip was trembling. Josie hugged her.

"Of course I do, sweetheart, but there are many different kinds of love. Now go and get ready for your date and I'll get ready for mine. I don't think that you've stopped loving me because you have a boyfriend."

Susie tried to say something else, but Josie stopped her.

"You're not going to change my mind, love. I want to do this for my own sake and you're going to have to deal with it." She went into the bathroom and by the time, she had finished her shower Susie had left the house.

Jas had done some research and drove straight to a quiet little pub on the way to Evesham. It was a very old building and the garden at the rear backed onto a river. The setting was idyllic and they sat facing the river and enjoying the beauty of their surroundings and the warm summer evening. Jas rested his arm along the back of Josie's chair as he told her all about his trip. After a while, Josie relaxed enough to rest her head on his shoulder as they watched the sun set against a rose-coloured sky. She told him about the scene with Susie, and how Susie had gone out without saying anything goodbye. He understood why this disturbed her.

"Still, at least it's out in the open now. I'm sure she'll get over it. She's not a child anymore." He said.

"I know, but we've always been so close. I want her to be happy for me."

"Then we have to show her we're serious. Come on, I'm taking you home. We should be there together when Susie gets in. Anyway, I have presents for you and Susie in the car and I can show you the rest of the photos."

It was still fairly early, not quite ten o'clock when they got back to the house. There was no sign that Susie had been back at all. Jas brought his laptop and some packages from the car, and while he was setting up the computer, Josie made tea. They sat on the floor, with the laptop on the coffee table in front of them. As the screen came to life, Josie saw her photo set as the desktop background and she felt a sudden surge of pride that he had chosen her. Surely, such an attractive, witty, charming man could have his pick of many women. She kissed his cheek. He set up a slideshow of the photos and sat with his arm around her telling her about each image as it came into view. When they reached the picture of Jas that he had sent to her, Josie leaned over and clicked on the "PAUSE" icon.

"Let me look at that one for a while." She said. "It's my favourite."

Jas laughed and kissed her. Then, handing her one of the packages he had brought in he said:

"You can have your present now, if you can tear you eyes away from your two-dimensional fantasy for a minute." There were two items in the package, the first was a midnight blue silk scarf with tiny silver stars scattered across it. It was a perfect match for Josie's favourite dress. The second was a red velvet box containing an exquisitely ornate gold crucifix on a fine chain. As Josie looked closely, she realised how unusual it was. The figure of Christ, so often depicted with his head bowed at the moment of his passing, was looking straight ahead and appeared to be smiling. His arms, stretched out in a gesture that seemed to offer an embrace rather than depict the agony that he must have been feeling. Josie thought it was the most beautiful crucifix she had ever seen. Turning it over, she saw that it was engraved with the words *"God is Love."*

"Is it OK? I thought of you as soon as I saw it."

Josie turned towards Jas and smiled as she put the chain around her neck. He helped her to fasten it. "I love it." She said, kissing him. "I'll never take it off. Thank you."

"First you love my clichés, and then you love my gift. I think we're we moving in the right direction."

Before Josie had a chance to say anything further, the sound of the front door opening alerted them to Susie's return. Rob was with her and they were clearly surprised to see Josie and Jas. It wasn't difficult for Josie to spot that Susie had been drinking. She was a little unsteady on her feet and rather giggly. Rob seemed to be quite sober and he steered Susie to a chair and perched on the arm. He saw Josie's concern immediately.

"I'm sorry, Mrs. Anson. It's not as bad as it looks. She's only had a couple of beers, but she obviously isn't used to it. I brought her home as soon as I realised it was going to her head." He seemed to be genuinely concerned.

Susie was looking at her mother cautiously, not sure what to expect. Finally, Josie smiled at Rob.

"You did the right thing. She's not used to it at all. Thanks for taking care of her."

She introduced him to Jas and then went to make coffee for everyone. Susie still hadn't spoken to anyone and Josie was apprehensive. She could hear the sounds of conversation in the living room but had no idea what was being said. She guessed that Jas and Rob were talking. They were both so polite and well behaved that they would be trying to act as if this evening's events were perfectly normal.

Returning with the tray of drinks, she found Jas showing Rob the photos. Susie had fallen asleep and Rob had moved down to the floor to get a better view of the screen. Josie took Rob's place on the arm of Susie's chair and stroked her daughter's hair while Jas answered Rob's questions about his trip. Every so often, Jas would look across at her and smile, and each time he did she felt her knees turn to jelly. On one of these occasions, she felt a tug on her arm and looked down to see that Susie had woken up and was looking at her tearfully.

"Mum, can we talk?" She said quietly.

They excused themselves and went into the kitchen. Susie threw her arms round Josie and cried like a baby while Josie patted her back and soothed her.

"I'm so sorry, Mum."

"It's OK, love. We've all had a bit too much to drink at one time or another."

"No, not about that. I mean about earlier. I was being so childish and selfish. I never thought about your feelings at all. I talked to Rob about it, and he laughed and said I was being silly. That's why I got drunk. I thought everyone was against me, but I was wrong. Can you forgive me?"

"Of course, darling. But what made you change your mind?" Josie was relieved beyond measure.

"I'm surprised you need to ask. You were watching them in there. I saw your face when he smiled at you. I feel like that with Rob. It frightens me sometimes to realise I can care so much about someone, but it's exciting too. Is it like that for you?"

Josie paused for a moment and looked at her daughter who was not a little girl anymore. She decided that the time had come to be completely honest.

"Yes, it's just like that for me too, and it's even more frightening at forty-three than it is at nearly-eighteen. Now let's go in and drink our coffee before the men decide they can manage without us."

Susie splashed cold water on her face and dried it on some kitchen roll and they went back into the living-room. Rob got up as they came in and put an arm around Susie.

"Everything OK now?" He asked.

"Never better," she said, and then to Jas "Can I see the pictures too?"

"Of course you can. Here let me show you your mum's favourite one first."

Josie protested half-heartedly.

"Jas, are you deliberately trying to embarrass me?"

"Yes darling, you're so cute when you blush." He teased. As the image came onto the screen, he winked at her and soon they were all laughing.

Later on Jas and Josie took the coffee cups into the kitchen to give the youngsters a chance to say goodnight. Jas was giving Rob a lift home. Once the door was closed, Josie threw her arms around him.

"You're wonderful. You've won her over completely." She said, kissing him passionately.

"You're wonderful too Jo. I'm glad we don't have to hide anymore."

Before leaving Jas gave Susie the present he had brought for her. It was a bottle of designer perfume. She was delighted and gave him a hug and then she and Josie waved goodbye as they watched him drive off with Rob. As they went back into the kitchen, Susie shocked her mother by saying:

"We should have got them to stay the night."

"What are you suggesting Susan Anson?" She was trying to look severe.

"Don't tell me it hasn't crossed your mind, Mum. It's certainly crossed mine. You'll have to face it sooner or later."

Josie turned away and started the washing up. This was a truly unexpected turn of events. Susie went to bed and a while later so did Josie.

Chapter Twenty-Eight

The next two weeks went by in whirl of activity. Josie was kept very busy at work with lots of requests for cards for June weddings. Of course, for her it was a labour of love. She enjoyed her work and she was able to see Jas every day. Although they were very professional at the office, the need for excessive caution had gone, so their special relationship was now an open secret. They went out for lunch together a few times and they double-dated with Pam and Karl twice. Josie was relaxed and happier than she had been for years.

The only cloud on the horizon was Susie's rapidly-approaching trip to France. Josie knew that she was going to find it very hard not to see her daughter for a month. She had promised Madeleine that she would go over for a weekend at the end of July for Susie's eighteenth birthday and she was looking forward to that. Still, she thought, things could be worse. Jas would still be here and they were having so much fun together. It was like being a teenager again – spending glorious evenings together that ended in long goodnight kisses, followed by tender phone calls in the middle of the night. Neither of them had spoken of love, which Josie found to be a relief. Once the word was spoken there might have to be changes; there might be expectations and she still hadn't overcome all of her obstacles.

The week before Susie was due to leave, she came home one evening in a state of high excitement. Josie was in the kitchen making a bedtime drink when Susie burst in.

"Mum, Rob's coming to France with me!" She sounded thrilled. "He told me tonight. He's booked his ferry ticket and everything."

"Have you phoned Granddad to make sure it's OK? Have they got enough room?"

"I phoned him earlier. It's all OK." Susie wasn't making eye contact with her and suddenly the penny dropped.

"I take it you'll be sharing a room then." Josie said. "You're a grown woman now and you can make your own decisions, but be careful Susie, don't get hurt."

Susie hugged her.

"I knew you'd understand. You're the best."

She understood only too well and in some ways she envied her daughter's courage. If only she could feel grown up enough to make her own decisions, life would be simpler.

On the Saturday of Susie's departure, Jas arrived at the house at six am. Susie and Rob were booked onto the lunchtime ferry and Jas had suggested that they should all go in his car because it was larger and more comfortable than Josie's and it would save Josie having to drive back alone. Rob had stayed over the night before to be ready for an early start.

It was raining as they drove out of Birmingham and onto the motorway heading south. In the back seat the two youngsters were animated for a while, and then they fell silent. Looking back Susie saw that they had both fallen asleep; Susie's head rested on Rob's shoulder and his arm was around her. They looked so happy.

"I'm really grateful to you Jas." She said. "I think I'd have been a wreck if I'd had to this by myself."

"No problem, darling. How often do I get to spend the whole day with you when we're not working? Besides, it's a lovely day for escaping from Birmingham. The weather down south is bound to be better."

They stopped for a coffee break at a service station and finally reached the ferry terminal with half an hour to spare. Susie turned back to wave as she and Rob walked away into the terminal and Josie waved back before turning to bury her face in Jas's shoulder and cry. He cuddled her for a moment and then they had to hurry back to the car to avoid getting a parking fine.

"Shall we get something to eat before we head back?" He said. "We've got plenty of time."

Josie nodded her agreement and after driving around for a little while they eventually found a parking spot in a small car park facing the Cathedral. The nearest pub offered lunches and they decided that would serve their purpose. It was called The Victory Arms. Jas was laughing and Josie asked him why.

"It's the name." He said. "I love the way Portsmouth is all about Nelson and HMS Victory, but it always amuses me because my name, my full name Jaswant, means victorious in Hindi. When I first came here as a child I thought it was really cool and I used to pretend I was called after the ship."

Josie laughed too, and told him that she had once seen a portrait of Joséphine de Beauharnais, the wife of Napoléon Bonaparte and had pretended to be the beautiful first Empress of the French. It had seemed so much more exotic than being "little Jo" who was named after her dad.

As they finished their lunch and exchanged more childhood memories, Josie's phone rang. It was Karl. Josie listened intently and then said:

"Thank you so much. I'll be eternally grateful to you." She ended the call and beamed at Jas. "It's over. Rick's letting me have the house as a 'clean break' settlement. He wants everything sorted out as quickly as possible. Apparently, Jess has been bending his ear about wanting to get married before the baby's born. Karl says it'll be finalised by the end of September."

"We'll have to celebrate your victory." Jas hugged her enthusiastically. "What would you like to do?"

"I'll let you know when I've made up my mind." She said. "But first of all can we go over to the Cathedral? There's someone else I need to thank."

"It's not a Catholic cathedral is it?" asked Jas.

"No, but it doesn't have to be. A prayer's a prayer wherever you say it."

Inside the vast cathedral, Josie knelt to pray while Jas marvelled at the architecture and the renovation work which had been carried out over centuries. Josie closed her eyes and gave thanks to God for the good things in her life. She prayed for Susie and Rob to have a safe journey. They would be almost halfway to France by now. Then Lee's voice was beside her, whispering in her ear.

"I'm off, Sis. Places to go, people to see and so on."

"Don't go Lee." She pleaded.

"I have to, my time's up. Anyway, you don't need me anymore. You know the truth." He seemed to be touching her shoulder. She could feel it.

"I don't know what you mean."

"Answer the question Sis. What is God?"

Then he was gone and she opened her eyes. Jas was sitting in the seat next to her. He was smiling.

"I thought you'd fallen asleep."

"No, I just..., never mind. I'm ready." They got up and on the way out, an old woman handed Josie a leaflet. They crossed the road to the car park and as they got into the car, Josie looked down at the paper in her hand. She gasped with surprise. Lee's words came back to her.

"Answer the question Sis. What is God?"

The leaflet in her hand proclaimed in large red letters. "GOD IS LOVE". She touched the crucifix that hung around her neck and bore the same words.

Josie looked at Jas and then at the leaflet again. Suddenly, it was all so clear. She laughed aloud.

"Jas, do you still want to celebrate my victory?"

"Of course I do. Have you decided what you want to do?"

"Yes." She said. "I don't want to go back to Birmingham today. I want to spend the night here."

Jas wasn't sure if she was serious.

"What? Right here?" he asked, laughing.

"No darling." She had never called him that before. "Let's get a room."

Chapter Twenty-Nine

"Where exactly are we going?" Josie asked as they headed out of the city. Jas didn't answer. He was being mysterious.

After she had surprised him with her suggestion about staying overnight, he had got out of the car and made a phone call. When he got back in he'd told her it was all arranged, but that they would have to do some shopping first, as he wasn't taking her to the sort of place where they could arrive without at least one overnight bag. Josie hadn't thought of this and was grateful that he had. It was true that nobody knew her down here, but she wouldn't have wanted people misjudging her anyway.

They had walked to Gunwharf Quays where they bought such mundane items as toothbrushes and toiletries. They had separated for half an hour in order to select personal items like underwear, as Josie said she would be too embarrassed to shop for lingerie with Jas in tow. When they met up again, Jas was carrying a small leather suitcase he had picked up in a charity shop. They had bundled their carrier bags into it and made their way back to the car park.

Jas was resolutely refusing to tell Josie where he was taking her, except to say that it was somewhere very special.

"If you won't tell me where we're going, can you at least tell me how long before we get there?" She asked.

Jas was in his element as he teased her.

"You surprise me, Jo. I had no idea you were in such a hurry. Relax; we'll be there in twenty minutes or so."

They drove through the New Forest and finally turned into a long and winding drive, flanked on either side by a glorious mixture of Canadian redwood trees and copper beeches, interspersed with rhododendrons. It was late afternoon and the sunlight sparkled on the leaves which still held raindrops from the earlier showers. Josie looked around her. The scenery took her breath away.

"Oh Jas. It's beautiful."

"Yes, and Heaven is just around the next bend."

The Forest View Hotel was indeed the closest thing to Heaven that Josie could imagine. As they rounded the final bend and the building came into sight she gasped. Originally a 19th Century manor house, it had been converted into a luxury hotel without losing any of its former character. Set in the heart of the forest it had beautifully laid-out gardens and terraces and a large ornamental lake. The building itself had features reminiscent of a fairytale castle. There were solid stone walls and turrets at each corner. Josie felt as if they were entering a different world as they got out of the car and made their way up the steps to the huge oak doors that were the main entrance.

A smartly dressed young man, with a rather supercilious manner, greeted them as they entered. He was wearing a badge that identified him as the duty manager. Jas gave his name and instantly the young man's attitude became deferential. He called the porter to take their case and then he personally escorted them in the lift to the third floor and presented Jas with the key to the Paradise Suite.

Once the manager had left them and the door was closed, Josie turned to Jas smiling like a child on Christmas morning.

"I said let's get a room, and you got us a palace!" She said, looking around in wonder at the Forest View's finest suite. It consisted of a huge sitting-room with soft leather sofas, a fridge and a TV, leading into a luxurious bedroom with ensuite bathroom. The king-sized, four-poster bed was draped in lilac silk. A number of deep purple velvet scatter cushions were arranged against the carved oak headboard. Everything about the suite was tastefully understated and yet the overall impression was of opulence and luxury.

"Is it a palace fit for the First Empress?" He asked.

Josie laughed with delight. "Oh, I should think so. But, I'd have settled for a tent on a beach somewhere as long as you were part of the deal." Now she was looking out of the window at a magnificent view of the Forest bathed in the golden evening sunshine. Jas crossed the room and stood behind her, his arms around her waist.

"So now that we're here, how do you want to celebrate?"

She leaned back against him and took his hands, guiding them upwards until they cupped her breasts.

"I want to feel victorious." She whispered with a smile.

He kissed the side of her neck and then turned her around to face him. "Let's see what we can do about that."

*

Two hours later, they had dinner in their suite and made love again. This time they went slowly, taking more time to explore each other. Josie realised for the first time just how inexperienced she was, as Jas found so many ways to give her pleasure. At the climax they came together, Jas having restrained himself until she was ready. She clung to him in the final seconds, crying and laughing as the waves of her orgasm swept through her body. She had never known it could be like this. Looking up into his eyes she could see that he felt the same. When it was over they kissed and lay curled up together as their bodies relaxed and their spirits returned from the heavens. Finally, Jas spoke shyly, almost tentatively.

"Jo, I haven't told you before, but I expect you know that I love you."

Josie's heart was so full at that moment that she thought it might burst.

"I knew, but I'm glad you've told me." She paused for a moment and looked into his chocolate bar eyes. "But did you know that I love you too?"

"Not until today, Empress. Then I knew. Today wouldn't have happened if you didn't love me. So I guess that makes us lovers now." He laughed.

"Fairly conclusive evidence, I'd say." She stretched out, relaxed and happy. Beside her Jas stretched too and yawned. She ran her fingers across his chest and he sighed.

"That's nice." He said.

"I could stop if you like and let you go to sleep." She teased.

Taking her hand and guiding it beneath the duvet he looked at her with a mischievous grin.

"Go to sleep?" he said. "Not tonight Josephine."

THE END

www.ingramcontent.com/pod-product-compliance
Lightning Source LLC
Chambersburg PA
CBHW020658030726
47498CB00002B/566